When It's Broke, It's Perfect

Angie Dowling

ISBN: 0615918859
ISBN-13: 978-0615918853

DEDICATION

To Trevor, Mark, Patricia, and Ronan.

This may be my first novel, but my life with all of you is my masterpiece.

CONTENTS

1 AN UNUSUAL PROPOSAL

"Jordan, I've come to a conclusion—I am never going to be able to be faithful to one woman. I've tried, and it's just not something I am capable of. I will never be able to just be with one woman; however, I truly believe that I could be faithful to two."

"Are you completely crazy?" Jordan Peck's head shoots up to look Chase DeWitt in the eyes. She gives him what she knows is her patented "are you messing with me?" look.

"Seriously Jordan," Chase continues, his blue eyes glowing. "I love Kendra, I really do. She's great! And our marriage is great. But it's just not enough. I need more. You've known me since college Jor...when have I ever really been a one-woman man?"

He has a point. An incredibly valid point. Jordan has seen Chase move from long-term relationship to long-term relationship, finally settling down with Kendra Barnes, now Kendra Barnes-DeWitt, and the only consistency in the last dozen years has been Chase's infidelity.

Chase continues, a wicked gleam in his eye. "Look at it this way—Kendra and I, we're an eight out of ten. Given how many people there are in this world, that's pretty damn good. But it's not perfect. If I find someone else who fulfills those other two needs, along with five or six of the things Kendra also embodies, by my math I am banking a fifteen or sixteen out of ten. I'm set!"

"Chase, you work as an editor, and words are your livelihood. Numbers are not. I'm pretty sure that your math is horribly flawed." Jordan laughs, because what he is saying is utterly ludicrous.

"I'm serious Jordan. With Kendra at home if I had someone ballsy, someone funny, someone like you, I could live out the rest of my days as a happily committed man," Chase replies, gesturing so dramatically that his shaggy brown hair falls over his eyes.

"You wouldn't be committed you idiot. You'd have your wife and your mistress!" The noise inside Al's, her favorite bar, seems to have risen dramatically in the last few minutes, so Jordan shouts in order to be heard.

Suddenly his last sentence processes through her brain. "Wait a minute…someone like *me*?" She winces at the way her voice cracks on that last word, and she feels a hot flush creep up her cheeks. She cannot believe this conversation is actually taking place. She's fought for years to keep feelings like this at bay.

She eyes him levelly, and tries to keep the nervousness out of her voice. "What do you mean, 'someone like me' Chase?" she begins. "There are plenty of women in the world, as your extracurricular habits have proven. Why in the world would you choose someone like me?"

"Are you kidding me Jor? You're smart, funny, you know more dirty jokes than anyone else I've ever met, and you've got a truly slamming rack!"

"Now is not the time to bring up my rack Chase," she shoots back. "Although, it is pretty spectacular," Jordan adds, laughing. In her mind though, she hopes that this joke will help change the tone of the evening. "Am I totally off my rocker, or did you just proposition me?"

"Jordan, I proposition you on average three times a conversation. You're just usually too dense to pick up on it." Chase is laughing now, but instead of breaking the tension, Jordan is even more unsettled. Maybe it is because of the way Chase's eyes keep raking up and down her body. She shifts her position on the black leather sofa, so that she is not full-on facing him, and is instead, looking sideways over her shoulder. She bites her lip.

"Chase, you know that *that* is never going to happen."

"*That* happened once before Jordan!"

"Dude, I was nineteen back then!" she exclaims, wishing he hadn't brought up the memory. Because it's true. A little over twelve years ago, Chase and Jordan had a one-night stand, born of tequila shots at a frat party and a dorm room poker game that got damn near X-rated, due to them being the only players involved.

Jordan shakes her head, clearing the memory, and

Chase's smile grows wider. "I know you're thinking about it."

"Shut up DeWitt," Jordan says, hoping he doesn't hear the waver in her voice. Normally the picture of composure, she feels completely out of her depth. "Besides," she adds, "you would do better to choose anyone in the world except me! I know all your secrets..." she trails off teasingly.

"That's exactly why you're perfect," Chase retorts. "You know me better than anyone else, even though we only see each other every other month." He looks at her, his expression softening. "Seriously though Jordan, you are absolutely fantastic. A guy would have to be blind and deaf not to know it."

"Tell that to my incredibly inactive dating life," Jordan smiles nervously. This conversation has veered off into difficult territory. Though attractive, with a trim but curvy figure, a choppy auburn bob, and bright green eyes, Jordan has always found herself to be "one of the guys," and developed a self-consciousness with men when it comes to actual romantic relationships.

She sighs, and continues. "You're sweet, and yes, that night was great, but that's not how I operate. I'm not anybody's whore."

"That's the beauty of this...I'm not looking for a whore. If I did, I'd be making time with the blonde in the low-cut top slamming Slippery Nipples over by the bar." He gestures towards a boisterous group of well-dressed women downing shots across the room. They are tall and thin, and in a way, remind Jordan of Chase's wife Kendra.

Jordan watches Chase watch the women, drinking

in his profile. His long, straight, nose, his full lower lip, and bristly lashes are familiar to her from years of friendship, but she cannot help but notice again how handsome he is.

Chase watches the crowd hoot and cheer as each drink is consumed, but then he surprises Jordan by wrinkling his nose slightly. He shrugs, looking for everything in the world like the cocky undergraduate he was back in college. "Maybe I'm finally getting old, but there's just not any appeal in that any more."

Suddenly his expression fades and he looks sheepishly nervous. "I want someone special. Someone who makes me happy. Someone I could even possibly love." He clears his throat, and then sighs. "But it is your call. I still think we could have something pretty great if you would just consider it."

Jordan stands up, pulls a twenty-dollar bill out of her pocket, and says, "I think this is my cue to head on out of here. This should cover my share of the drinks."

"You don't have to..." Chase begins, and it is Jordan's turn to sigh.

"I really do Chase. I'll see you later."

Chase stands, his six-foot-four frame dwarfing Jordan, even in her four-inch heels. Before she can slide away, he envelops her in a big bear hug, the kind that they have always shared, the kind of hug that hasn't felt awkward in years, but feels unfamiliar now. He kisses her cheek, tenderly, whispering "Just think about, would you Jordan? For me?"

"Goodnight Chase." Jordan turns and walks out of the smoky bar, fumbling for her keys. She steps out into the balmy June air, and takes a deep breath. Her walk is a little unsteady, not because of the beers, but because as much as she doesn't want to admit it, will never admit it to another living soul, Chase DeWitt has given her a *lot* to think about.

2 TWELEVE YEARS AGO

"Let's do another!" shouts Jordan over the pulsating bass of the Outkast album that has been *the* party soundtrack her sophomore year.

She is riding what students at her small liberal-arts university snidely refer to as a "scholar's high". After a semester filled with Russian literature, art appreciation, Eastern philosophy, and intermediate French, she is ready to cut loose. Final exams are over, the summer looms bright ahead, and she has secured straight A's for the first time as an undergraduate. She is indestructible, and she is ready to celebrate.

"Are you sure you can handle another tequila?" asks Emmy, her neighbor and best friend.

"Emmy, tonight I think I can handle just about anything...even him," Jordan replies as her eyes dart across the crowded fraternity house basement towards freshman Chase DeWitt. Both girls watch him as he takes a sip of his beer, followed by a long, slow drag of a cigarette.

The sheer sight of DeWitt, as he is known to his fraternity brothers, and the shape of his mouth as he exhales a cloud of smoke, is enough to send a shiver down her spine. They have shared a semester of Dr. Wright's philosophy class, a few cigarettes, and several brief conversations, and while Jordan has always found him attractive, she has never acted on it. Never even voiced her attraction to anyone besides Emmy.

"Chase DeWitt?" Emmy laughs. "He's only a freshman. And he's way too tall for you Short Stack. Plus I heard he just got out of a relationship like fifteen minutes ago." Her face reflects the amusement and skepticism in her voice.

Jordan snorts derisively then giggles to cover it up. "For starters, I'm nearly five-foot-seven in these shoes." She wiggles her three-inch heels with a wry smile. "Second, he's less than a year younger than us, so get off that high horse. And lastly, he and Tara have been broken up for at least two weeks, and from what I hear, it wasn't that serious."

"People say it wasn't that serious because he was slutting it up with half the Delta Gamma pledge class behind Tara's back!" Emmy retorts. "*Ewwwwww…*" she squeals, shuddering. "There is *no* telling where that boy has been Jordy."

"He *is* a little trampy…"

"That's like saying water is a little wet sweetie."

"Well it's my life Emmy, and I think a little bit of bad behavior is well-earned at this point," Jordan answers back, playing with her necklace nervously.

"With that kind of logic, you sound like a true

English major. You can justify any argument, no matter how ridiculous," her friend answers, laughing. She eyes Jordan warily before throwing her hands in the air. "I give up. I know that look too well. You're going to do whatever you damn well please, and there is nothing I can do to change your mind."

Jordan smirks as she continues to adjust the silver pendant around her neck. "You're exactly right," she retorts, grinning. "Here goes nothing," she cries as she grabs their refilled shot glasses and turns away.

"Hey! That's mine!" Emmy is shut down by Jordan sauntering away, one shot glass in each hand.

She approaches Chase DeWitt casually, her heart pounding beneath her black tank top. She has admired the freshman with the lanky, tanned frame and shaggy brown hair for months, but has never expressed her interest, largely because of his rumored Lothario status. While she is undeniably attracted to him, she doesn't want to be just another notch on his dorm-room-issued bunk bedpost. Her feelings for Chase transcend the physical. Chase is articulate, witty, and likable. All semester long Jordan has been impressed at his insights in class, and for her, there is nothing sexier than intelligence.

Suddenly, she is next to him, and determined to not look foolish. "How'd your exams go Chase?" she asks carefully, trying to mask the butterflies.

"Oh hey Jordan!" Chase smiles at her, his blue eyes warm and friendly. "I guess they went pretty well., but Wright wasn't crazy about my final paper, in which I condemned the yin-yang sign as currently being nothing more than a superficial symbol of modern philosophic pretension. Nabbed all A's except for him. B-plus." He smiles again, a slow grin, his eyes taking in her shoulders, her collarbone, and the faint suggestion of cleavage visible at the neckline of her tank.

"Not too shabby for a first year!" Jordan isn't surprised, but is nonetheless impressed. Professors are notoriously tough on freshmen, believing that harsh academic criticism is part of the collegiate acclimation process.

"How'd you fare?"

"My ideal poker hand." Chase looks at her quizzically.

"Four aces!" she exclaims, laughing. Jordan grins, because as lame as it may seem to some, she is proud of her accomplishment.

"Nice work Jor!'" he declares, extending an open palm for a high-five, as he registers the shot glasses in her hands. "Whoa, it looks like you've got your hands full. Is that rum?"

"Tequila." She smiles wickedly at him. "Here, do a shot with me," she says, extending the plastic shot glass to him. He takes it from her, his eyes zeroed in on her mouth.

"You know, they say that tequila makes people do some crazy things," he says, raising an eyebrow.

"Well then here's to some crazy things," she laughs, clinking her tiny plastic cup against his. They smile at each other before tilting their glasses back.

"So you play poker huh?" Chase asks, as he pulls another cigarette from the pack of Marlboro Reds tucked into his front pocket.

"Yeah, I've gotten into it recently, and not to brag, but I'm getting pretty good."

"Cool. So are you a big gambler? Do you bluff a lot, or do you only play if you have the goods?" Chase smirks as he asks this, obviously suggesting more.

Jordan is not clueless to the subtext. "I like to keep people on their toes." She smiles at him coyly, reaches out for his cigarette, and takes a deep drag. Exhaling slowly, she smiles slyly at him. The liquor has made her bold. "What do you say I show you just how I play?"

His eyes light up and his gaze once again goes to her cleavage. "I like your style Jordan. How about we take this game upstairs to my room?"

While she wants the immediate satisfaction, Jordan wants this on her terms, which includes not sleeping with Chase DeWitt during a raucous frat party, with dozens of people right outside their door. "I have a better idea. How about we take it to my room? I have a single on the Lower Quad."

Chase's smile spreads wide and he reaches down to cup her face with his hand. "Beautiful, brilliant, and no roommate? Jordan Peck, you might just be the perfect woman." He leans in and kisses her slowly.

"Let's get out of here."

***

The stumble back to Jordan's room is unmemorable, but when Chase squeezes her hand as they navigate the dirt trail, she knows she will never forget this moment. The feeling of his warm hand wrapped around hers gives her chills.

They get back to her room and Jordan mixes them each a rum and Coke from the stash in her desk drawer. Jordan grabs a desk of cards off her desk, and gazes at him as she settles down on the floor, marveling at her incredible luck. For months she has imagined being alone with him, and now it is actually happening.

Chase sits cross-legged, across from her, on the multi-colored shag rug she chose to protect her feet from freezing linoleum on winter mornings. She deals a hand of Texas Hold 'Em, and waits for him to make a move. Chase holds his cards in front of his face, partially obscuring his smirk. He has an excellent poker face, as he has worn the same smug grin since walking through the door.

The first few hands they play for fun, but after twenty minutes of trading wins back and forth, they are all business. They are playing with the quarters from her laundry jar, but as Jordan started to deal the hand, Chase half-whispered mischievously, "How about the loser forfeits an article of clothing each hand?" Jordan, dumbstruck and more than a little tipsy, can only shrug and nod her consent.

She glances at her cards. King-five, a hand she adores with the sentimental affection usually felt for a troublesome pet. On the floor and ace, a king, a seven, and an eight are showing. One card left.

Chase bets fifty cents, the minimum bet. Jordan knows it is possible, even likely, that he holds can ace, but tonight, she feels like luck is on her side.

"I call," she says, tossing her coins into the pot. She flips the last card, a five, and suppresses a grin. "Check or bet?" she asks him.

"I check," Chase replies.

"I bet a dollar fifty," she responds hesitantly, as to not betray her hand.

"Call! Prepare to lose Jor," he says defiantly, as six quarters land into the small mountain of coins between them. *I cannot believe Chase DeWitt is about to get shirtless in my room,* Jordan thinks to herself. He flips his cards over.

"You have got to be kidding me!" Jordan blurts out, as he shows a king and a five of his own. She turns her cards over, laughing. "I guess it's a split pot. Neither of us is losing anything."

"Bullshit!" Chase counters. Then a wide grin spreads across his face. "I say we both lose something."

"I suppose that's fair," she admits. "On three then. One, two—" and Chase has already whipped off his t-shirt, revealing his slim-built but toned chest.

She has been waiting, hoping, for this moment all night. All semester. All school year, if she is being honest with herself. "What are you waiting for?" he asks teasingly. He once again lets his eyes wander to her cleavage.

Jordan hesitates for a moment then, eying what Chase so casually put on display, the small thatch of brown hair between his pectorals, she grasps the bottom of her tank top and deftly pulls it over her head, exposing her black, strapless, bra.

"Now *that's* what I'm talking about!" Chase responds. The way he is looking at Jordan makes her instantly feel as though she has taken off much more than just a tank top.

"Oh come on," she admonishes him. "It's basically the same thing as a swimsuit, for crying out loud. Besides, it's your deal..." she tells him, trying to refocus on the card game.

"Screw the game," Chase answers, tossing the deck aside. He reaches across the pile of unclaimed quarters, takes her face in one hand, as the other moves to her waist. "Come here," he murmurs huskily, sliding a finger into one of her belt loops and pulling her close. Coins slide beneath her as he tilts her face up to his and kisses her firmly, sweetly, his lips perfectly soft and firm at the same time.

Jordan allows herself to be pulled into his lap, her legs wrapping around his muscular back. She shivers as she feels his tongue slide between her lips, as Chase's hands move up to her hair, gently tugging at her long brown locks, his fingers wrapping the strands.

Their kiss lasts for what feels like an eternity. Jordan pulls away, smiling broadly, and stands up, taking his large, strong hand in her small, silver nail-polished one. She leads him to her bed, where she sits "Are you sure you want to do this?" Chase asks her, nervousness present in his voice for the first time. Though his voice wavers, his eyes are burning into hers, his desire apparent.

"Yes, oh god yes..." she whispers, and this time, it is Jordan who pulls him in for a kiss.

3 HAUNTED

Jordan opens her eyes a crack, as she fumbles for the phone on her nightstand, trying to shut off the alarm. It seems like eight in the morning keeps coming earlier and earlier, especially after the restless nights of sleep she has gotten these last few nights.

Chase's proposition, the only word Jordan can use to describe it, has been weighing on her mind ever since Saturday. Last night she dreamed of that night her sophomore year. She and Chase had shared a night of passionate sex, filled with kissing, touching, and exploring in ways Jordan had never experienced before, and has rarely encountered since.

She remembers waking up that morning after their hook-up; her head nestled in the crook of his arm. He kissed her forehead and arose from the bed. He programmed her number into his cell phone, promising to call her later. After dressing, he gave her one last sweet kiss, and left, and Jordan couldn't shake the dark feeling that she wouldn't be hearing from him.

She did hear from him, but in the worst way possible. The next day, late in the afternoon, after a day and half of anxiously waiting, she got a call from him, in which he clumsily explained that he had gotten back together with Tara the afternoon after he'd left her room. He told her that she was "an awesome girl" and that he didn't want to lose her friendship, but he was firm that the events of "that night" couldn't happen again. He repeated how important it was to him that they stayed friends, and all she could muster was a casual-sounding "sure thing" that she hoped masked her disappointment.

Though she knew going into it that Chase DeWitt was as unreliable as he was intelligent, and that his predilection for fooling-around was school legend, even as a freshman, Jordan Peck could not help but feel disappointed by the way things had gone down. She harbored no regrets for the night she had spent with his, but she was definitely wounded as a result.

Luckily, summer vacation had started after that. Jordan was one of the few students left in the dorm, a benefit of having secured a position as a counselor for the camp that was housed out of the university each summer. The campus cleared out over the next few days, Chase went home to Louisiana, and she spent the summer running writing workshops for high school students and slowly putting herself back together.

By the time Chase returned to campus that August, Jordan was able to resume a friendship with him. It was tentative at first, but grew, slowly, into the connection they shared today. Jordan and Chase might not talk but once every week or two, usually through text or Facebook, but over time they started getting together for drinks every month or two, and they became each other's confidantes, secret-keepers, and trusted allies.

This particular morning though, Jordan wishes that Chase didn't share with her quite so freely. His openness, his ability to lay his desires out on the table, has always slightly mystified her. Jordan has always considered herself to have a firmly grounded sense of right and wrong. While her youth was absent of church or religion, her parents raised her on the principal of "be kind to others," and Chase's repeated infidelity has always fallen into the category of Unkind Behavior.

He has always explained it to her with the grace of the liberal arts scholar they were both trained to be, stating that morality "was a social construct, the invention of man; and therefore subject to reinterpretation or even outright dismissal, as determined by the individual," a line Jordan is convinced he lifted from an old college paper. For years, he has argued that individual work and individual satisfaction were the only true obligations a person possessed.

As long as Jordan has known him, Chase's quest for personal satisfaction has led him into bed with a seemingly endless string of women. He has drifted from relationship to relationship, with little time in between. And in each of those relationships, he has been faithful for only a few months, either beginning trysts that evolved into his next girlfriend, or more recently, indulging in one-night-stands when out of town on business.

When Chase told her he was going to marry Kendra Barnes, she thought it might be the end of his wandering eye. However, six months after the ceremony, Jordan received a late-night text, bragging about a new conquest. Since then, it has been more of the same; every couple of months, he's got a new story to tell her. He swears that he is always very up-front with the girls he sleeps with, making them well-aware that it is purely sexual, but Jordan can't help but think back to that night in her dorm, and the tender passion that transpired between them, and feel a sense of pity for those girls.

And now he wants her to be his constant conquest! Jordan shakes her head vigorously, finally pulling herself out of bed, stumbling towards the kitchen.

Her favorite thing about her apartment, which she has shared for the last five years with Emmy, her friend since college, is the kitchen. Airy and spacious, it is a rarity in Atlanta complexes. She shuffles to the coffeemaker and puts a large pot on, knowing that Emmy will be up soon, and heads into the shower. A nice, hot, shower and strong cup of black coffee are just what she needs to get her head on straight and get on with her day.

Jordan is an adjunct professor of literature, a position she secured after earning her Master's degree directly after finishing her undergraduate studies. Luck, as well as her strong networking skills, earned Jordan her current position, as the university she teaches at usually doesn't employ anyone without a PhD. However, over the last three years she has secured her place as a tough but encouraging professor, and she is poised to move to the tenure track once she completes the doctoral work she plans to start next year.

Today is a busy day. Jordan has two classes to teach, as well as an extended block of office hours, during which any number of students will come in to discuss their writing, ask questions about texts, or seek her advice on the personal matters that students seem to bring to English teachers far more frequently than those of other subjects. Her course load this semester is intense but intellectually invigorating: two introductory level courses, "American Literature 1850 to Present" and "American Drama", and her first special topics course, in which Jordan was able to select a central theme and develop a semester-long curriculum around it.

She chose "Sexuality in Fiction," a topic that seems more than a touch ironic in light of recent events, but it remains the highlight of her week. It is an upper-level course, available only to students with at least sophomore standing who have taken at least three previous literature classes at the university. Her class contains only fifteen students, small even by the standards of the exclusive institution at which she is employed.

She begins her teaching day at 9:30 with her American literature class, takes a short break for lunch, then moves right into her 12:30 Sexuality in Fiction class. The current text is Vladimir Nabokov's *Lolita*, and though it is early in the book, her students are already struggling with the challenging wordplay and often mystifying narrator.

***

"The trickiest part of Nabokov's work is the fact that we can't rely on our narrator to be honest with us," Jordan tells her Sexuality in Fiction class later that day. "He's highly introspective...the entire novel is essentially a personal reflection of his actions, his crimes. Yet, we have to cautiously analyze his every confession. Humbert is a criminal: a child molester and a murderer. "

Her students listen with rapt attention, jotting notes diligently as she continues. "Let's examine this early passage from Chapter 4:"

"When I try to analyze my own cravings, motives, actions and so forth, I surrender to a sort of retrospective imagination which feeds the analytic faculty with boundless alternatives and which causes each visualized route to fork and re-fork without end in the maddeningly complex prospect of my past."

She looks at Avery, a strong student with whom she has discussed this section during office hours. She finds it always beneficial to start a discussion with a student who she knows is capable of intelligent commentary. "Avery, can you tell us what Humbert is explaining here?"

Avery, ever the teacher-pleaser, even at twenty-one years old, is eager to explain. "Professor Peck, what he's saying is that when he tries to reflect on his actions, even the really bad ones, he gets so lost in his own past that he never really is able to come to any conclusions."

"Very good Avery. Humbert is telling us that he basically gets lost in his own backstory, second-guessing his actions, playing an endless game of 'what if' that in no way offers up any easy answers to the reader. It is for this reason that we as readers must be hyper-critical, as it becomes our responsibility to determine these answers, because Humbert sure as hell isn't giving it to us."

The class snickers as they do any time she swears in class, a practice she only indulges in with upper-level students. Her freshmen come in so indoctrinated by high school rigidity that they would absolutely lose it to hear that kind of language from a professor. This is why she loves teaching this course: the students are motivated and interested, and there is an overall air of maturity she hasn't been able to experience in other classes.

Jordan continues, "there is much discussion of Humbert's childhood within the early phase of the novel. What event does he hold as the main 'cause' of his later-in-life compulsions that cause him to embark on a sexual relationship with an adolescent girl?"

Abby, a soft-spoken sophomore, raises her hand. "Well, I think that Humbert never gets over his first love, and that's why he chases young girls all his life. It's because he never got to..." Abby trails off, as a blush spreads across her cheeks.

"It's because he never got to 'culminate' his relationship with Anabel," Jordan says, rescuing the girl, who is clearly struggling with the sexual nature of the text. "His initial, fledgling sexual relationship is cut off before it's time, and because of that, he spends the rest of his life trying to fill that void. He longs to 'finish' the matter, a hopeless wish, as the object of his affection is dead."

Jordan thumbs through the text, shifting little piece of index cards that mark annotated passages. She reads another selection aloud to the class:

"All at once we were madly, clumsily, shamelessly, agonizingly in love with each other; hopelessly, I should add, because that frenzy of mutual possession might have been assuaged only by our actually imbibing and assimilating every particle of each other's soul and flesh."

She addresses the class: "In this passage, Humbert describes his first love as so intense that he would only be satiated by literally consuming her and integrating her soul with his. Now tell me...is this a realistic depiction of first love, or just further evidence that Humbert is, as he describes himself, a madman?"

Avery raises his hand and answers, "I think it's unrealistic. I mean, on a basic level, his expectation is completely out of bounds. You can't, at least in most societies, eat a person, and if you did, it would end the love affair pretty quickly."

Jacob, an insightful senior, rebukes him. "Take the gross literal interpretation out of it Avery. What he is basically implying is that, no matter what, we never really escape our first love. The worse it ends, the more we are horribly scarred by it. Humbert is more screwed than most, because there is no hope for resolution—no chance of a happy ending. All he has is a lifetime of chasing an unattainable ideal."

Jordan is impressed with Jacob's insight, but his comment has struck a nerve, and she feels a wave of uneasiness wash over her.

Is that why I am still feeling so mixed up inside about Chase? Jordan asks herself. *Is that why I am dreaming about that night sophomore year? I'm thirty-one for crying out loud.*

The class has taken a turn for the personal, and she is nervous about navigating the waters of this discussion without divulging too much about herself. "So Jacob, do you believe that Humbert is right? Are we doomed to forever suffer the slings and arrows of our first love?"

"Well, sure. I remember my first love. I think in some ways the nature of our relationship affects how I treat women today. But Professor, you've got more experience than us..." he begins, before flushing crimson and beginning to stammer. "I'm not saying that you're old, or that you've been around or anything, but...I mean, it's only logical to assume that you..."

Jordan can't help but laugh. "Yes Jacob, I would wager that I have more life and relationship experience than most college students. I would agree with you to an extent. I think that our earliest amorous relationships color our later romances, but I think that the extent varies based on the nature of that first relationship, the personality of the individual in question, and the cumulative experience acquired since that first encounter."

At that moment, Chase's face blazes across her mind, his self-confident smirk appearing just as it did that night at the end of her sophomore year. She swallows, and continues. "I mean, I know people who, at fifty-three, are screwed up in the head by relationships they had when they were twenty-three. I guess it works the same way. If you don't process it, you don't move past it. However, we are quickly running into territory that I am sure the Psychology department would come down on me for how blasé I am in analyzing this subject matter. Also, we appear to be out of time for the day. Have the rest of part one completed for Thursday, and for the love of god, be highlighting and annotating as you read. Humbert's overall psychological state and unreliability as a narrator are the key concepts. See you then guys."

Her students file out in small clusters as Jordan collects her papers and heads upstairs, her head swimming. *I'd say my attempt to distract myself was a pretty spectacular failure*, she thinks to herself as she climbs the spiral staircase to her office.

Her office is small, as befits an adjunct professor, and drafty, but to Jordan it is a symbol of her accomplishments. She has worked hard to prove herself at the university, and now she has a Special Topics course, her own office, and the promise of greater things ahead. If only she could take her mind off of Chase DeWitt.

When a professor holds office hours, it is something like educational Russian Roulette. Sometimes there is a line of students awaiting her and sometimes, like now, it is desperately quiet. After checking her email and organizing her notes for her lectures the rest of the week, Jordan is ready to head out. She quickly writes "Professor Peck has cut office hours short today. Please email her if you have any questions that can't wait until Wednesday" on a blue sticky note, places it squarely in the center of her door, and heads out.

As she slides into her green Honda Civic, Jordan thinks to herself, *Work wasn't enough to distract me, and*

I clearly can't do it myself. Maybe I need to bite the bullet and talk to someone who might understand. She starts the engine, cranks the air conditioner, and before pulling out her parking spot, pulls out her phone. She sends a quick text to her roommate:

Need your advice on something. Meet me at home in an hour?

Almost immediately her phone chimes in response: "Sure". Jordan smiles at the hope of finally getting some insight, and leaves the school. As she makes her way home, she stops off at the grocery store for a six-pack of beer. While she knows her roommate will give her good advice, Emmy can be blunt, sometimes painfully so, and Jordan knows this conversation will go down much easier with a drink in hand.

4 SNAP JUDGMENT

Emily Trew, known to Jordan simply as Emmy, sits on the sofa with her friend. Jordan came home about twenty minutes earlier, carrying a case of beer, a sure sign that she's nervous about the "talk" she requested earlier in the day.

After being friends with Jordan for nearly a dozen years, Emmy knows her friends actions as well as she knows her own. While Jordan has never been a particularly heavy drinker, whenever she is "too" something: angry, excited, nervous, or some other high-intensity emotion, she will have a drink to loosen up her tongue. For someone who usually dives right into controversial debates, and who often seems downright bullheaded, Jordan has always had an incredibly difficult time expressing her emotions in times of conflict.

It seems as if tonight is one of those nights, because as soon as Jordan walked in the door she made a beeline for the kitchen, opened a beer from the twelve pack in her hand, and placed the remainder of the case into the fridge.

Since then, Jordan has proceeded to nurse her beer while engaging Emmy in small talk: stories from her lecture today, and questions about some of the clients at the non-profit women's shelter that Emmy has been running for the last five years.

This is another hint that whatever Jordan needs to talk about is making her nervous. When she's got good news to share, she tends to blurt it out instantly. It is only when she fears the response that she becomes reticent. Furthermore, for the last few minutes, Emmy has watched Jordan carefully peel and shred the label from her bottle of beer, another of her traditionally nervous habits.

"All right Jordan, what's on your mind? You've been acting weird since you walked in, so just spit it out already."

Jordan looks up at Emmy, only for a moment then resumes intently working on removing the label from her bottle. The main label lies in tatters on the coffee table, and she is now concentrating on detaching the band around the neck.

"Well you know I went out with Chase last weekend."

"Yes, and I have no idea why you still associate with him. He's even shadier now than he was in college!" Emmy blurts disgustedly, cutting Jordan off.

"Knock it off Em. He's my friend," Jordan says, narrowing her eyes, letting Emmy know she means business.

"Fine. Well, what did he do now? You've been off for days, and I can only guess that cree — that Chase is somehow involved."

"Well, we were having a great time just catching up. I was telling him about my classes this semester, and he was talking about some new clients he just landed, when things just go...weird..." Jordan trails and bites her lip. "He basically, I mean, what he said...he implied that—"

"What Jordan? Just say it for crying out loud!" Emmy practically shouts at Jordan, anxious to know what it was that Chase DeWitt said to unnerve Jordan so much. She's never understood the friendship between the two of them, ever since he treated Jordan so callously back in school.

Suddenly, Jordan blurts out the whole story. "Well, he said that he doesn't think that he'll ever be able to be totally faithful to Kendra, but that is he had someone consistent on the side, he'd be able to be satisfied and happy," she confesses, her eyes darting around the room nervously, landing everywhere but on Emmy.

"He said WHAT? Are you kidding me?" Emmy responds shrilly. Though this is the kind of behavior that she expects from a low-life like Chase DeWitt, she's stunned and appalled that he actually had the nerve to say it out loud.

"It doesn't end there Emmy. After telling me all that, he basically admitted that he wants me to be the 'other woman' in his life."

"I hope you told him to go to hell!" Emmy replies. "Does he even realize that he's married? I mean, it's bad enough that he slept around on every freaking girlfriend he's ever had in his life, but he's got a wife! A. Wife. That's a vow. People shouldn't take shit like that lightly!"

"I know that you feel that way Emmy. Please just let me finish," Jordan asks.

"I can't imagine what you could say, or what he could have told you to justify that kind of nonsense," Emmy snaps back. "I've told you before about the kind of destruction that this kind of a man can create. You of all people should understand what kind of pain he can cause. After the way he treated you last time, how could you even think of..." she trails off. "It's just completely reprehensible!" she states, changing her focus.

Emmy's fired up now. While she has always been personally repulsed by the lies and deceptions that come with infidelity, the transparency of Chase's declaration has left her utterly disgusted. Every day at the shelter she sees women come in absolutely destroyed, physically and emotionally, by narcissistic, self-serving men like Chase DeWitt. Emmy has her own, more personal reasons for condemning Chase's behavior, which she has never explained to Jordan. For a moment, she considers confessing her secret to her friend, but instead shakes her head angrily.

Instead, Emmy launches into a tirade about the selfishness of men "like Chase" and the destruction they inevitably cause to good women. She talks while Jordan gets herself another beer, talks while Jordan begins to shred that label as well. Emmy talks until Jordan stands up and declares that she has a ton of grading to get to and excuses herself to go work in her bedroom.

In fact, Emmy talks for so long that she never actually asks Jordan whether or not she is actually considering his offer. It is only later, when she is getting ready for bed, that she realizes Jordan never stated a plan one way or another.

Still, as Emmy climbs into bed and pulls up the covers, she does her best to push her doubting thoughts out of her mind. *There's no way,* Emmy tells herself. *Jordan could* never *do something like that.*

5 CAN'T SHAKE THE THOUGHT

Sitting in his plush office in downtown Atlanta, surrounded by all of the trappings of a successful life, Chase DeWitt is troubled. Less than two weeks ago, he went out for drinks with Jordan Peck, an old college friend, and he had a plan. He had an idea, a brilliant idea, which would neatly tie up the various loose threads in his life. He wanted, he still wants, to bring Jordan into his life in a big way, to reignite an old relationship they had abandoned over a decade earlier.

At the end of his freshman year of college, he and Jordan had a one-night stand. A night of flirtation and intimacy so intense that it still creeps into his dreams, even at the age of thirty-one. He's been with many women since then, but he's never been able to completely remove her from his thoughts.

Even though he has been with his wife Kendra for five years, married three, Chase has never been faithful. Ever since college he has been unable to shake the powerful temptations that cross his path. And indeed, it did start in college. When he arrived on the campus of his small, liberal arts university at the age of 18, he felt like he was being reborn.

In high school, Chase DeWitt was a geek. Tall and scrawny, with a straight-A average, the only thing keeping him from being the stereotypical image of nerd was the absence of glasses and a pocket protector. He even sported big metal braces until halfway through his senior year.

The summer after graduation changed all that. He spent the summer lifeguarding and playing Ultimate Frisbee, a schedule that gave him some much-needed down-time, muscle definition, and a healthy color to his previously pale complexion. All of this sent him off to college feeling the best he had ever felt, looking the best he had ever looked.

Once at school, he focused on reinventing himself. He pledged a fraternity, developed a taste for both weight training and beer, and at the insistence of his frat brothers, even allowed his previously perfect grades to slip to B-level.

For the first time in his life, he felt strong, confident. Under the tutelage of Greg Osborne, his big brother in Sigma Chi, he had learned how to talk to women, and to his surprise, the women were responsive. Very responsive. Greg encouraged him to play the field, telling him that he was young, and need to enjoy "a taste of the strange" as much as possible.

He dated around for the first semester before settling into a relationship with Tara, a pretty blonde in his freshman core class in January. They dated for months, but when faced with flirtation from other girls, including Tara's sorority sisters, he would crumble. So, he snuck around in secret, until finally, he decided that his infidelity was the result of not really being serious about Tara, at which point he broke up with her, a few weeks before spring finals.

That's where Jordan came into the picture. Though they had shared a philosophy class together all semester, and had noticed her wide smile, green eyes, and edgy style, he had never been certain whether or not she was attracted to him until the night of The Post-Finals Bash. She had approached him at the Chi Phi house, armed with two shots of tequila, her smile a come-on that needed no interpretation or analysis.

They got together, and it was incredible. Every way that they moved, they were perfectly synchronized; there were no bumped noses or clashing teeth that night. It was a perfect night, but when it was over, he felt the need to escape. He watched Jordan, arm curled up under her head as she slept, he knew he couldn't jump into another relationship, and he especially couldn't bring himself to hurt this girl.

When Tara called him the next day wanting to talk, and eventually proposing that they get back together, he relented. In his mind, if he couldn't be faithful to Tara this time, it wouldn't really be that big of deal, as he had already cheated before. However, by the time he returned to school after a summer at home in Louisiana, he and Tara were off again, and Chase was firmly committed to enjoying a life free of romantic commitment.

After that he sailed through the rest of college,

generally enjoying life, and sleeping with the many women who made themselves available. He eventually drifted into a long-term relationship with Amanda, staying faithful for nearly three months before straying. This pattern continued throughout his twenties, until he met Kendra Barnes, a beautiful girl who was the epitome of everything that geeky Chase could have never gotten in high school. But even Kendra wasn't enough to keep him faithful.

By the time Chase got married, Greg and the rest of his college friends had largely settled down. The night of Chase's bachelor party, his big brother had pulled him aside and said "Alright Chase, you've had a hell of run. Now it's time to stop screwing around and grow up." His words had filled Chase with a deep chill, which he attributed to cold feet and quickly dismissed. Though he stayed faithful to Kendra for the first year of their marriage, he knew in his heart that he wasn't yet ready to give up his "taste of the strange," and he eventually fell back into old habits.

The only thing to his credit is his discretion. Though Chase has cheated many times, with many women, none of his girlfriends or his wife has ever had any idea what he has been up to. He is truly cautious, having made a promise to himself that no one would ever be hurt in his affairs. This is about fulfilling his needs, satiating an inescapable desire deep within him, and nothing more.

Though Chase knows that what he was doing would be considered by many to be wrong, he truly can't help himself. He loves the pursuit, the back-and-forth of flirtation, and the excitement of a woman other than his wife.

This is why he went into his outing with Jordan so gung-ho. In his mind, he has created the perfect solution. He can have Kendra at home, sweet, elegant, gentle Kendra who would never hurt a fly, whose biggest flaw is being predictable.

In his plan, he also gets Jordan, who is brunette, feisty, funny, outspoken and stubborn, refusing to yield her ground in a fight. He would have everything, and he believes he would be sated. He has enough time, enough stamina, and even enough room in his heart for two women, provided that the second woman was as easy to talk to and care about as Jordan Peck.

However, Chase knows that the likelihood of him getting his perfect ending is slim to none, as he recalls the appalled look on his friend's face as he outlined his plan. He has confided to Jordan since his junior year, long after their night together, and over the years, she has become the only person he tells about hook-ups, flirtations, and affairs. He was so certain that she would be the one to understand his needs, and that their connection was so deep that she would instantly see the beauty in it.

Now, Chase feels burdened and alone, without anyone to help him puzzle out his thoughts and identify where he went wrong. Usually, this is the point in his day where he would pull out his phone, text Jordan, and let her pragmatic attitude put him on the right track. Knowing that's impossible given the circumstances, he dials the next-best thing. After two rings, a familiar voice answers.

"This is Greg."

"What's happening big brother?" Chase exhales a sigh of relief. Greg helped Chase find his confidence as a freshman, and if anyone can help him figure out how to proceed from here, it is him.

"Chaser, bro, how's it going?" Greg sounds happy to hear from him. It's been several months since they've spoken, but as it often goes with male friendships, they pick up as if no time at all has passed.

"Pretty good man. How are Erica and the kids?" Chase spouts the appropriate small-talk, anxious to get to the point where he can vent about his own problems.

"Can't complain my friend. My boy started kindergarten a few weeks ago, and little Lily is walking and getting into absolutely everything." It still stuns Chase to hear this guy, his idol and his Yoda rolled into one, wax enthusiastically about children. Every time Kendra even mentions children, he is ready with a list of excuses why the timing isn't right, because the fact is, he can't imagine bringing a kid into the world. Greg continues, "but I know you didn't call to talk about my kids, so what's on your mind little bro?"

"Well, I've got a problem I've been struggling with for the last few weeks, and I was hoping maybe you can help me out. You see, there's this woman…"

"Stop right there man, I'm not getting into this garbage with you. I thought you outgrew that whole man-whore thing when you walked down the aisle."

"Hey wait," Chase tries to interrupt.

"Don't give me that Chase. You committed to Kendra in front of all of your family and friends.

Doesn't that mean anything to you?"

Chase can hear the disappointment in his big brother's voice, and it only makes him more frustrated and despondent.

"Greg, this is different," he argues. "I'm trying to find a balance, to find peace..."

"So you're still invoking the core curriculum of our *college* to explain your terrible decisions. Have you changed at all since you graduated?"

Greg's words sincerely hurt Chase. He knows he sounds ridiculous, maybe even pathetic, but he genuinely wants to settle the urges that have driven him from woman to woman since his late teens. In his freshman year of college, he was required to take a two-part series of classes on the self, and how the individual creates a path for themselves as they seek fulfillment, and since then, he has been preoccupied with the idea of his own fulfillment, of being truly satisfied.

Greg's words, calmer now, break the awkward silence. "Listen Chase, it's time to grow up. Whoever this girl is, and trust me I *don't* want to know the details, she can't hold a candle to Kendra."

"But—" Chase begins, before Greg cuts him off again.

"No buts, because even if you think she's the greatest girl you've ever met, even if she does things you've only seen in movies, she's not your wife. Kendra is, and if you screw this up, you'll regret it forever."

Chase exhales slowly, knowing that their conversation is at an impasse. "You're right Greg. I know what I need to do, and I know everything will work out. Thanks for helping me get some perspective."

"I'm here for you Chase, as long as you quit being such an idiot," Greg laughs, convinced that he has managed to get through to his erstwhile little brother.

"Talk to you later man, bye." Chase hangs up the phone, and feeling more confused than ever, stares out the window for several minutes.

He reaches for his cell phone, still warm from use for his call to Greg, and opens a text message. He's got no choice but to reach out to the one person who always understands him, even if right now she is at the center of his problem.

Need to talk to you. Drinks Friday at the bar?

He puts the phone down on the desk, and busies himself checking emails. Nearly ten minutes pass before his phone chimes in reply. It immediately goes off again, signaling a second message.

Roommate out that night. Just come over.

See you then.

Smiling to himself, Chase DeWitt returns to work.

6 BOILING POINT

Jordan checks her reflection in the mirror, taking a moment to fix the part in her angular asymmetrical bob. She's expecting Chase any minute now, and she wants to feel confident.

She has changed her shirt twice, moving from a cleavage-baring top to a simple fitted t-shirt the same shade of green as her eyes. She doesn't want to look too dressed up, wants to keep things casual, but she derives strength from feeling put together.

She's still unsure what exactly she will say to Chase when he arrives. When he texted her the other day, she was a little surprised. She feels a lingering sense of awkwardness from their last conversation, but she and Chase have always been honest with one another, and she doesn't want that to change.

Even though she doesn't want him to think she's making herself available to him, she checks her makeup one last time, and adds a quick spritz of her favorite perfume.

Suddenly, there is a knock at the door, and all of her careful preparation, her determination to appear cool and collected, flies right out the window.

She walks to the door and lets Chase inside. He's carrying a twelve pack of beer, and Jordan can't help but smile.

"You always show up prepared, don't you DeWitt?"

Chase smiles, slowly at first, eventually breaking out into the wide grin she knows so well. Just having him nearby makes her feel calmer, an effect he has had for years now. As they settled into the confidante relationship they've nurtured since college, he has always been able to make her feel more peaceful. She still feels the current of nervousness, but it's a quiet hum as opposed to the intense roar she was feeling just minutes earlier.

"Hey, it's rude to show up empty-handed when you've been invited over," Chase laughs. "My momma raised me right."

Jordan lets out a snort of laughter. "Seriously? You're going to try to use that old-school simple Louisiana boy routine on me? I think I know you better than that. Especially after how two weeks ago you basically said you want to bone me."

With one bold reference to the previous week, the easygoing conversation between them grinds to halt. Chase's smile drops, and Jordan sees that he's nervous, an emotion he never displays, perhaps just as nervous as she is.

"Listen Jordan, about that..."

"Don't worry about it Chase. Let's just pretend it never happened," Jordan says, anxious to try to move the conversation along. "You caught up on *Walking Dead*? I've got the most recent few episodes on my DVR still. We can watch some while we drink up your hostess gift," Jordan laughs nervously.

"Stop Jordan. Just stop it." Chase's reaction is instantaneous and intense, taking Jordan by surprise. He takes a deep breath, calming himself, and continues. "I don't want to sweep it under the rug Jordan. We've never done that before, and I refuse to start now. I tried to tell you something last week, and I messed it all up. Can we please just hang out for a while, have a couple of beers, and then, maybe, just maybe, I'll be able to explain myself a little better."

Jordan is momentarily stunned. Her friendship with Chase has, ever since their one-night stand, been fueled on easygoing humor and sarcastic jokes. To hear him speak so earnestly to her takes her by surprise.

"I think I can handle that Chase," she finally replies, smiling hesitantly. "How about we get started on those beers man?"

"Great," he says, opening two beers and handing one to her. "So, how are your classes going? Busy molding an eager batch of young minds?" he asks teasingly, as they sit down next to each other on Emmy's black leather sofa.

"That pretty much covers it. In addition to my usual course load I have my first special topics class 'Sexuality in Fiction,' and it's providing some pretty interesting conversations. You know me; I can't stand to make it easy on them, so we've started with Nabokov's *Lolita*."

"Are you serious? That book is beyond messed up.

Humbert is a total trainwreck."

"That's the challenge!" Jordan laughs. "Humbert is a pervert and a pedophile, but he's also incredibly damaged. The classes in Russian literature that I took as an undergrad are seriously paying off. I'm trying to make sure that they see that a damaged and immoral character can be compelling, and even weirdly sympathetic, if you look past the surface actions and you look at the events that drove them to such an unhappy and desperate place."

"I see what you're saying, but Humbert is a calculating and deliberate man. He's a predator. How do you perceive him as deserving of sympathy?"

"He does immoral things, but it's all driven from a point in his childhood where he essentially winds up in a state of arrested development. He's a middle-aged man, but no more developed than a teenager." Jordan cocks an eyebrow and gives Chase a sideways look. "How do you know so much about Nabokov anyways?"

Chase grins widely, before answering, "Actually, I took the Introduction to Russian Lit class my senior year. I had a blank spot in my schedule, and this really cool chick who had graduated the year before was crazy for the Russians, so I decided to see what all the fuss was about."

Jordan blushes, realizing the implications of what he has just said. "You took a class because of me?"

Chase takes a deep drink from his beer. "You really don't get it, do you? Anytime you speak, I'm listening. You are without a doubt one of the smartest, most interesting people I've ever met. I could listen to you talk like this about literature for hours. I can see why your students love you so much."

Jordan can feel her already warm cheeks flush even deeper. She looks up at him cautiously. "You mean that man?"

"Jordan, I've never meant anything more sincerely."

She takes a deep breath and steels herself to ask the question that has haunted her since she was nineteen. "Then what the happened back then?"

Now it's Chase's turn to redden. "What do you mean?"

"That's crap and you know it. What happened my sophomore year? Why did you get back together with your ex-girlfriend basically the same day after we got together?"

He exhales deeply. "I was young and stupid. Girls never looked at me before college. Then when I got to school, it seemed like they never stopped looking. It was the most incredible thing I'd ever experienced, and I genuinely couldn't help myself. The girls were there, and I felt like I was missing out on something by not going for it."

"This sounds awfully self-pitying for a guy who has screwed up so much of his own volition."

Chase hangs his head as he sinks onto the couch next to her. "It's the truth Jor. God I remember lying in bed with you, holding you and thinking to myself 'Don't you dare screw this up.' So I bolted that morning. I figured I would just wind up hurting you, so when Tara wanted to get back together, I guess I convinced myself it was better to risk cheating on a girl I'd already been unfaithful with, rather than cheat on the most incredible woman I'd ever met."

Jordan puts her beer down on the table and reaches up to cup his face with one hand.

"You're a total idiot Chase DeWitt," she says, slapping him playfully on the cheek.

He laughs in spite of the situation. "I know that. I've done a lot of incredibly shitty stuff to a lot of women over the years, but the way I treated you, and how amazing you were, forgiving my sorry ass, that's the one thing I've ever felt truly guilty about."

"I need a second," Jordan interrupts. "Want another beer?" He nods, so she heads to the kitchen to get them both a refill.

"You okay?" Chase asks, as Jordan settles herself onto the couch, tucking her feet up.

She sighs, and nods. "I'm fine. I'm just so confused. Why did you never say anything over the last twelve years? You've been single since then, so why did you never approach me again until now?"

"Honestly, I didn't think you'd even consider it. I spent nearly a month working up the balls to tell you what I did the other week."

"So where does Kendra fit into all of this?" This question is perhaps even harder for Jordan to ask. She bites her lip nervously.

"I meant what I said last week. She's great, but it's just not enough. I've been with other women since we got married, but nothing has ever calmed me down for long. I constantly feel restless. The only time I ever feel…calm…is when I am with you."

"Chase you're married and what you're telling me is that you have every intention of staying that way, but you still want to start something with me?"

"I know it sounds insane, but you give me something I've never felt with anyone else. I feel like if I don't at least try, I will regret it forever," he says, moving to a standing position, pulling Jordan up with him.

Jordan feels his arms wrap around her shoulders, pulling her close. "I don't know if I can do this Chase...I think I want to try. It's just that I've never been in this kind of situation at all. I've never cheated...never even considered it..."

Her words are cut off by the immediacy of Chase DeWitt's kiss. As his lips touch hers, she can feel one hand move up to her hair, even as the other holds tightly to her waist.

Jordan feels a little unsteady, but finds her body responding to his involuntarily. She has wanted and waited for this for so long, as hesitant as she is to admit it. She presses herself against him and allows her lips to part, deepening their kiss.

After a few minutes, Jordan manages to pull herself away and catch Chase's gaze.

"So what are we doing here exactly? Is this just going to be a repeat of before? Are you just getting something out of your system?"

Chase places a hand under her chin and gently leads her gaze up to meet his. "Jor, I don't *want* you out of my system, and I don't think I could get over you even if I tried. It's different this time. *I'm* different. Everything will work out."

Jordan looks into his bright blue eyes and again bites her lip. "I hope you're right Chase," she murmurs, kissing him again.

The two settle back down on the couch, where they

slide back into conversations about work and stories about the students and clients who make their lives more interesting.

Suddenly Jordan gasps. "Shit!" she swears, "Chase, I think I may have made a mistake. The other day, I was so stressed, and to try to work past my feelings, I confessed to Emmy what you had said."

His bright smile fades, but Jordan continues. "She absolutely cannot know that you've even been over here, let alone that we…"

"We what? Kissed?" Chase teases, tracing her cheek lightly with one finger. "Kissing's not a crime Jordan. Emmy can get off her high horse and get over it."

"Be serious," Jordan replies, her expression darkening. "She's absolutely opposed to 'the way you are' when it comes to women, and if she knew that we were doing…" she trails off, blushing once again. "…if she knew that we were going to be doing, what I am pretty sure we're going to be doing pretty damn soon," she continues, as she starts to toy with the buttons on his blue and white checked shirt, "It would be safe to say she would absolutely flip out. I can't even imagine how bad it would be. I mean, we're on her couch. There is a one-hundred-percent chance she would lose it completely."

Chase laughs gently, and then plants small kisses up and down her neck. "So where's Saint Emmy tonight anyways? Every time I see that girl I think she's about to kick me in the balls."

Jordan suppresses a giggle, a response to the light touches Chase is administering as much as at the mental image of Emmy and her Doc Martens taking a shot at Chase.

"She's at a fundraiser for the shelter. It's supposed to go until after midnight, and since she'll stay to supervise clean-up, she won't be home until close to two."

"That sounds like we have plenty of time then." Chase smiles, and in a moment of reverse dejá vu, takes her by the hand, and leads her to the bed.

7 FEELING THE EFFECTS

"Chase, wake up baby," a voice whispers to him.

"Huh? Oh hey Kendra," he replies as his wife's face comes into focus. He sits up in bed and shakes his shaggy brown hair.

"Good dreams honey?" she asks brightly. "It's nearly ten. You never sleep this late."

"I guess you could say that. I was also out pretty late with the guys last night. They must have put me through the wringer worse than I thought!" he laughs easily. Truthfully, he got in after one in the morning, and his dreams were all repeats of the previous night with Jordan.

After years of wanting and waiting, they finally connected again, and for Chase, it was the most spectacular sex of his life. While he is aware that part of it may have been the forbidden aspect, he knows that most of it was simply the connection between the two of them.

While he has always remembered their one night

together in college with fondness, nothing could prepare him for the intensity of the previous night. It began with kissing in her living room then he led her to her bedroom, where he slowly undressed her. There was no need for pretenses like poker this time. He deliberately removed her shirt, then bra, drinking in her smooth pale skin before moving lower to unbutton her jeans.

There was no awkwardness, no tentative exploration of each other's bodies. They seemed to move instinctively, kissing, touching, and after much foreplay, consummating the desire that had, in truth, been building since they were teenagers.

He watches Kendra walk over to their bedroom window and open the blinds. Sunlight pours into their room, reflecting off of the pristine white bedding that Kendra has chosen to decorate their room, blinding him for a moment.

"Jesus Christ Kendra, can't you ease a guy into it? Or at least hand me a pair of sunglasses first?

"Oh don't be such a baby. Go hop in the shower. We've got brunch plans in an hour," she replies teasingly. "Move your butt lazybones," she adds, taking a gentle swipe at him.

"Okay, okay, I'm up," he groans. He makes his way to the bathroom and turns the shower on full blast. A soon as the water is hot, he steps inside, hoping that that the steaming stream of water will help clear his head. As incredible as his night with Jordan had been, it wouldn't do to have his head clouded with thoughts of her all day long.

***

Brunch with Kendra, and one of her giggling friends, Melanie, he thinks, had been relatively painless, but as Chase settled down into his office, his thoughts again drifted to the previous night.

While the rest of the house had been decorated by Kendra in a combination of whites and bright floral prints, this room was the one space that Chase has declared as purely his own. It is filled with dark wooden furniture with navy blue leather upholstery, mirroring both the fraternity house that was so pivotal in his formative years and the pub he frequents now.

It is in here that he does much of his work. He has worked for years to rise from a lowly copy writer for a company that provides website content for many area businesses. As he advanced, being given more editorial duties, the firm expanded into national markets, and he has finally become the person in charge of all deals in the southeastern part of the country. As a result, he has the cachet of being able to work from home when the mood strikes him, going through the copy his underlings produce, searching ruthlessly for errors.

Though he is the youngest editor, he is perceived as a bit of a wunderkind within the company, being able to spot mistakes in grammar and weak turns of phrase and rework them into copy that truly pops and engages the reader.

While he told Kendra that work is what draws him to his office, and it often does, tonight he has retreated to his own personal sanctuary searching for clarity.

Throughout brunch, he was unable to fully remove Jordan from his thoughts. His mind keeps going back to the feel of her soft hair, the shine in her deep green eyes as she moved in close to kiss him.

When he left, it was torturous. He made sure to pry himself away in time to avoid interruption from her judgmental roommate Emmy, who in his opinion, had been insufferable in college and has since evolved into a creature of such self-righteous piety that he sought to avoid her at all costs, even before he and Jordan began their affair.

For Chase knows that this is far more than a one-night-stand or a fling. He's walked that road before, and this is something completely different. The night before Jordan called him out on his callous behavior when they were in college, and it cut him to core.

He wants to prove to her that he is different this time. He's not just a dumb kid who doesn't think things through. He wants to show Jordan Peck that he is serious about creating something real and lasting with her.

While part of him knows that he is being unrealistic in his expectation, that he's married, and he does truly care for his wife, but he cannot resist the pull. He knows that he wants Jordan, physically and emotionally. He wants to have many, many more nights like the one before, and he wants to make her feel safe and secure, to make her feel how deeply he cares. He wants to keep her as an important part of his life for as long as he possibly can.

He pulls up the internet on his computer and clicks around to a few of his favorite sites, humor pages that range from dick jokes to social satire and everything in between. Still Jordan is on his mind.

Suddenly, inspiration strikes him, and he knows

exactly what website to go to, and exactly how he can show Jordan his true feelings.

8 OUT OF CHARACTER

"Dammit!" Jordan swears as she shuffles papers around on her desk, searching for her notes for today's class. While part of her feels that she can conduct the day's lecture with just her highlighted copy of the text, her notes have become her security blanket, and she just feels more confident when they are in hand.

She spots a few sheets of notebook paper, lifts up a stack of freshman essays, and heaves a sigh of relief.

Notes in hand, she heads down the tight, spiral, staircase to room 302. As always, her students are waiting, novels out, notebooks open to a fresh sheet of paper.

"Good afternoon everybody!" she greets them cheerfully. "Everybody ready to get their learning on?"

Her class chuckles in response to her deliberately

dorky greeting as she drops her belongings on the desk at the front of the room. She opens her copy of *Lolita* and immediately launches into her lecture.

"So last week we essentially concluded our analysis of the first four chapters, so today we will move onto five. In this chapter, Humbert begins to in great detail explain his fascination with 'nymphets,' the root of said fascination having been explained in the prior chapter."

She watches her students as they begin to scribble, and smiles. This is where she always feels the most confident; leading a discussion about a book she truly loves.

"For example, what is Humbert saying when he claims, 'I was consumed by a hell furnace of localized lust for every passing nymphet whom as a law-abiding poltroon I never dared approach. The human females I was allowed to wield were but palliative agents?'"

Jacob is once again among the first to throw a hand in the air. She nods at him, giving him permission to answer.

"Basically he's saying he's a fetishist." The younger students in the class giggle at his choice of words, still occasionally uncomfortable by the sexual frankness that is at the core of the course.

"Okay calm down guys," Jordan commands her students. "Jacob, explain your logic."

"Well, it's pretty simple. He speaks of his incredible desire to bed these young girls, and it's only his fear of the law that keeps him from attempting to do so. Furthermore, any 'appropriate' sexual relationship he seeks, meaning of course sex with a partner his own age, is basically a quick fix to a bigger problem."

"You have the essence of it correct Jacob. Humbert has a very specific desire, and anything else would basically be a Band-Aid on a gaping flesh wound." Jordan stops and looks around the room, watching her class frantically scribble her words.

It always amuses her how much her students try to write down every phrase out of her mouth. She wants her students to get the big ideas of the literature, but when it comes time for them to write papers, students who parrot back her thoughts instead of crafting their own will inevitably score lower.

Suddenly there is a knock on the door. Jordan's eyes dart to the window, where she sees a uniformed delivery man.

"Give me a second guys, let's see what he needs," she says as she moves to the door. She opens it, and he steps inside, carrying an elegantly arranged display of colorful lilies in a simple black vase.

"Excuse me, this is a classroom. I think you may have the wrong location. Perhaps you are looking for one of the offices, or a student dorm further down campus?"

"No, the ticket says Professor Jordan Peck, Harper Hall, room 302. That's this place right?" the delivery man replies. "You must be Professor Peck. These are for you," he continues, brandishing the beautiful arrangement.

Instantly, he class breaks out into a chorus of "ooooohs" that make them sound infinitely more high school than college. Jordan, blushing, tries to quiet her class with a sharp look, but it is obvious from the pink in her cheeks that she has been caught off guard and her students know it.

"Who are they from Professor?" Avery asks.

"Yeah, did you get a *boyfriend* and not tell us?" Jacob quips, with a wicked gleam in his eye.

"Oh hush, all of you. I have no idea who they are from," Jordan responds, and it's true. No one has ever sent her flowers before, and as she reaches for the card, she can't help but feel a rush of excitement. Her hands tremble as she opens the envelope and pulls out the tiny card inside.

The message reads: "We all have those people we never get over right? Thinking of you, Chase."

Jordan again feels her face flame with giddy embarrassment. "Rest easy guys, they're just from my parents, congratulating me on putting up with the bunch of you," she quips, trying to change the subject.

A dozen pairs of arched eyebrows tell her that her explanation was perceived as the obvious cop-out that it was.

"Let's get back to the topic at hand: Humbert's preoccupation with his nymphets. He acknowledges that he could potentially have a societally acceptable relationship when he says that, 'Humbert was perfectly capable of intercourse with Eve, but it was Lilith he longed for.' Imagine for a second that you are friends with Humbert, or god forbid, you have the misfortune to be his therapist. What do you say to him?"

Abby is the first to respond. "I'd tell him that even though he feels these things, he has to resist them, because they are explicitly morally wrong."

Jacob cuts her off, "That's only because you and

Humbert are both products of the modern American-European era. If you had been in a different culture, or born a hundred years earlier, the problem would not exist. Girls as young as Lolita were frequently married to men of Humbert's age."

"But that culture and era *are* what Humbert has been born into, and he needs to respect the boundaries outlined by both," Abby retorts, lifting her chin defiantly. "Based on the societal paradigms outlined in Humbert's world, what he wants is wrong, and as such, we need to respond critically to the events that are going to unfold."

"Hey the heart wants what the heart wants, right Professor Peck?" Jacob replies. "Isn't that the lesson at the core of all of this? Even if we know that it is morally wrong, we are all wired a certain way, and that's just the way it is."

"That's one attitude Jacob, and certainly one that Humbert would employ to his advantage. However, as the events of the novel unfold, we will see the consequences of Humbert pursuing what his heart wants. Your perspective may change. Be open to that possibility, just as you Abby," Jordan continues as the young girl's heart jerks up and she focuses her attention on the professor, "you need to be open to the idea that Humbert could just possibly win you over. That's the greatest challenge we face as readers."

She pauses, before adding, "We have to be willing to accept whatever the author throws at us, and continually adjust our judgments as we read."

Jordan shifts the class discussion to a later part of the chapter, and the rest of the class moves along smoothly. However, in the back of her mind, Chase's gesture and Jacob's words work in conjunction to give her butterflies in her stomach. *The heart wants what the heart wants,* she thinks to herself, smiling. The Chase DeWitt of old would never have made such a significant and public gesture. *I guess I just need to see where this goes.*

9 UNDER PRESSURE

Kendra Barnes-DeWitt looks at her watch anxiously. Four-fifteen. It is conference week for her first-graders, and her last appointment for the day is running late. She's already stressed out from the day and looking forward to her evening plans of a yoga class and drinks with friends.

She deliberately scheduled this conference for the end of the day, knowing it would go long past the twenty-five minutes usually scheduled. Trey, a bright but inattentive child, is not thriving in her class, causing worry and frustration for both Kendra and the boy's parents.

She checks her email and, seeing nothing, begins reviewing her lesson plans for the rest of the week. A few minutes before four-thirty, as Kendra starts to pack her bag to leave, a frazzled-looking woman who can only be Trey's mother bursts into the room.

"Mrs. Barnes-DeWitt?" the woman asks, and Kendra nods. "Traffic was a nightmare, I am so sorry.

Is it too late for our conference?"

"Not at all," Kendra replies, her sweet nature concealing her frustration. She pulls out her iPhone and quickly texts her husband.

Conference running late. Going straight to yoga, then out with the girls. Home around 11. Love U!

She sits down at the table with Trey's mother and begins pulling work samples out of his portfolio.

Forty-five minutes later, after a conference twice as long as any of her others this year, Kendra is finally ready to leave. She grabs her phone out of her desk, and sees a message from Chase.

K. U2.

Wow, she thinks, *that's brief, even for him,* as she shuts off the lights and pulls the door closed behind her.

***

Kendra moves into Sarvangasana, her toes pointed straight to the ceiling, legs extended elegantly, and holds the pose until her instructor tells the class to release. She slowly lowers her legs, and then moves to a standing position. After bowing to her instructor, she takes a quick drink from her water bottle, rolls up her mat, and packs her gear neatly into her light pink yoga bag.

"Kendra!" She hears her name and turns abruptly to find her friend Melanie looking at her curiously.

"Sorry Melanie…what's up?

"I called your name like three times. You were completely spaced out!" Melanie laughs cheerfully.

"Whoops! I guess today's session left me *really* relaxed! Are we still on for tonight?"

"Absolutely. Showers first though. I feel like a sweaty hot mess." Melanie eyes Kendra, and continues, "But look at you! Not a drop of sweat. I am totally jealous." Her friend's curly brown hair is damp with sweat, and tendrils are escaping her tidy bun.

Kendra shrugs casually. "I guess I just hide it well. First we shower, then we'll head out."

After getting cleaned up, Kendra gazes into the mirror, reapplying her makeup. Her face is tanned and smooth, her sky-blue eyes set off by the artful braided bun she has pulled her still-damp hair into.

She applies bronzer with a puffy brush, then rims her eyes lightly with a silver pencil. A quick coat of mascara and a sweep of lip gloss complete the look. She smiles hesitantly at her reflection, not wanting to appear overly pleased with herself, especially next to Melanie, who is sighing with frustration over having to cover blemishes.

"For crying out loud, I'm almost twenty-seven! Why does my skin still break out like a teenager," Melanie huffs, applying a second layer of concealer. "Don't you ever have this problem?"

"Good genes, I suppose," Kendra says gently. "You look great. Let's hit the town."

***

The rest of the group is already there when Kendra and Melanie arrive at the wine bar. This is the place for their weekly gatherings, Kendra and a group of girls she has known since college. They were all pledges in Chi Omega freshman year, and have remained fast friends for nearly a decade.

Melanie is a petite, curvy brunette whose insecurities often mask her keen intellect. Often quieter than the rest of the group, she is Kendra's reliable best friend, and has provided her with much advice and laughter over the years.

Aubrey and Becca, willowy women with perfect blow-outs who are often mistaken for sisters, despite the contrast between Aubrey's olive skin and black hair and Becca's strawberry blonde locks and generous freckles. They were roommates from freshman year until their weddings four years ago. The ceremonies took place only two weeks apart, their dreams of a joint ceremony dashed only by the "selfish" insistence of their husbands.

After their weddings, the two women settled into similar sprawling suburban homes not more than 3 miles apart. They are both now associates at the same law firm in downtown Atlanta, with a conjoined plan to become partners in that firm by the age of thirty. They are well on their way, already known throughout the building as "The Dynamic Duo."

Alicia is a light-skinned African American beauty who married a player for the Atlanta Falcons in a decadent ceremony that her friends deemed "a bit much" behind her back. Already a mother of two, her "work" consists of heading a charity affiliated with the team, though much of her day is dedicated to the gym and her elaborate "personal maintenance" regimen, while the nanny watches after her children.

For better or worse, these are Kendra's nearest and dearest friends. She loves them passionately, and as she settles into a plush velvet armchair next to Alicia, she can feel her spirits rising.

"What's new ladies?" she asks as she reaches for the already-open bottle of chardonnay and pours it elegantly into a chilled glass. This greeting long ago became an inside joke, as any major development in their lives is instantly broadcast to the group via text message.

Alicia smiles wickedly. "Apparently there *is* some news to announce, because these two," she smirks, gesturing at Aubrey and Becca, "haven't lifted a glass since they walked in."

Kendra gasps and her eyes dart to their empty hands. "Oh my gosh! Are you…" she trails off.

Aubrey and Becca beam nearly-identical perfectly white smiles. "We're pregnant!" they declare gleefully before dissolving into giggles.

"That's great! Congratulations!" Kendra replies instantly, though she can feel her stomach drop, knowing what is coming. "How far along are you guys?"

Aubrey begins, "I'm ten weeks—"

"—And I'm twelve!" Becca crows. "This brat," she says, elbowing Aubrey in the ribs, "may have beat me to the altar, but I'm going to beat her to the cradle!"

Kendra raises a finely-plucked eyebrow, and warns, "Careful Becca, or Aubrey is going to have that baby early just to spite you!"

They all burst out laughing, as Aubrey mimes a boxing stance and pretends to land a blow on Becca's shoulder, careful to avoid her still-taut midsection. Alicia takes a sip of her wine then cocks her head in Kendra's direction. "When are you and Chase finally going to get on the wagon?"

Kendra blushes, and stammers, "Well, Chase and I,

we've talked and, it's just not the right time for us..."

"Oh lay off Alicia!" Melanie interrupts. "I've still got no one! Let's work on finding me a man before you push Kendra into your 'Stroller Club.'"

Kendra shoots Melanie a grateful glance, and mouths a discreet "thank you" to her friend, who simply nods in response.

The "Baby Issue," as Kendra considers it in her mind, has been a bone of contention in her marriage for the last year or so. She and Chase began their relationship on a deliberate trajectory. They met six months into her senior year of college, as she was completing her student teaching, at which point Chase was already three years into his career as an editor. They married a year later, bought a townhouse in an up-and-coming section of Atlanta, and both began to rise through the ranks in their respective fields. Chase became the managing editor for Digital Promotions, as Kendra settled into a position as the lead first grade teacher at one of their county's top elementary schools.

For Kendra, the logical next step is children, yet every time she mentions it, Chase has reasons to postpone. His current excuse is that he feels like neither or them is really ready to throw away their freedom, to go "full-domestic." While Kendra sees his point, it is beginning to feel like an empty excuse.

"Kendra!" Becca calls her name sharply, snapping her out of her thoughts. "Aubrey and I were just saying that we want to do a joint shower right before Christmas, before we all leave for the beach." The annual New Year's Eve trip south has been in place for the last five years. Each year the girls pick a destination, and always, their boyfriends, fiancés, and husbands are always all too happy to follow.

"Sounds great!" Kendra replies enthusiastically. "I'd be happy to host!" She pulls out her phone, and briefly notices that Chase hasn't texted, then immediately begins typing ideas into a note file. "So do you two want a couples' shower, or have it be just the girls?"

"We'll see the boys all that next weekend. Let's just have it be us, a few girls from the firm, and the rest of our pledge class," Aubrey answers, instantly letting Kendra know that this will likely be a party of at least 20 women, as Aubrey and Becca's definition of "a few" usually means "approximately ten" and their pledge class consisted of an additional dozen women beyond their core group of five, all of whom have stayed in Atlanta post-college, and who all, even now, jump to socialize with "the cool group" that Kendra and her friends have dominated since they were all eighteen years old.

"Sounds *fabulous!*" the two mothers-to-be respond in unison.

"So you guys are going to find out the gender ahead of time right?" Melanie asks. Becca and Aubrey respond as a pair, and Kendra, knowing that the scrutiny has shifted away from her childless state, feels her shoulders relax as she settles in for a long session of chit-chat, gossip, and laughter with her closest friends.

10 JEALOUSY RISES

Chase's phone vibrates angrily, notifying him that he has a message. He rolls over, kisses Jordan's stomach, and retrieves the phone from her nightstand. A few quick swipes of the keypad, and he checks his messages.

"Sweet!" he exclaims. "Looks like I get to stay until ten or so. She's going to yoga and then out with her friends." He is cautious not to say Kendra's name in front of Jordan. A month in, and she is still visibly uncomfortable at the mention of his wife.

"You know I've got grading to do," Jordan replies, stretching her limbs out like a cat. She reaches for her shirt, and pulls it on.

Chase smirks at her. "At least let me make dinner for you before you throw me out, he pleads winningly.

Jordan sighs, and tilts her head up to smile at him. "Your idea of cooking usually involves a take-out menu, doesn't?"

Chase puts a hand over his heart, southern-bell-style. "Good heavens whatever gave you that idea? I'll have you know that I made a perfectly *marvelous* toaster waffle."

"You're a mess," she giggles in response. "So what's it going to be, Chinese or pizza?"

"Chinese of course! Only the most exotic of the take-out cuisines for my lady," Chase simpers as he pulls on his pants.

Jordan shakes her head, laughing. "There's just no fixing you is there?"

"I yam what I yam and that's all that I yam," he mugs, *Popeye*-style. His tone shifts back to its usual baritone. "So what do you want?"

"General Tso's please, with steamed rice," she replies.

"Spicy, just the way I like my women," he quips, pulling out his phone to call for food.

Jordan rolls her eyes, and as Chase steps into the other room to place their order. She looks around her room, at the various articles of clothing strew across the furniture and floor. Chase's boxers lay crumpled in the corner by the door, and her bra, flung across the room in a fit of passion, manages to land on her desk chair. Her sheets are rumpled and twisted, and the pillows have been knocked to the floor.

Jordan begins to straighten up the bed and collect the debris from around the room, laying the clothing across the now-neatly spread sheets. As she works, her thoughts go to the choices she has made.

Whenever she is with Chase, she feels stronger, lighter, and more alive than she ever has in her life. That intoxicating effect he possessed as a student has only increased with age. His smiles, laughs, and touches send shivers up her spine.

The problem, she thinks to herself, *is when we're* not *together*. The longer their affair, for she knows deep in her heart that's the proper term for it, continues, the more easily she is able to compartmentalize her guilt. Chase is quick to tell her that their time together should just be enjoyed, not overanalyzed, but Jordan has never been one to shy away from introspection.

The morning after that first night at her apartment, Jordan woke up to a wave of guilt and shame. However, Chase's thoughtful gesture a few days later helped to calm her anxiety. As much as she understands on a basic level that what they are doing is wrong, Chase brings a level of joy to her life that she is absolutely unable to turn away from.

Though Jordan drinks, she has never done a single drug. But she understands now what an addiction feels like.

A few minutes later, order restored to her bedroom, Jordan walks out into the living room to check on Chase. He is stretched out on her couch, watching television, his bare feet propped up at one end. He smiles as he sees her and asks, "What's shaking? Food should be here in twenty or so."

"Sounds great, I'm absolutely starving," she replies, taking a playful kick at his feet. "Move your feet weirdo, you're in my way." He swings his long legs in front of him, and she plops down onto the couch.

Chase gently places his hands on her shoulders and begins to knead her muscles. "Jeez girl," he remarks, "Why so stressed? You'd think after the last hour you'd be completely relaxed." Jordan can feel him smiling behind her as his hands begin to work out the knots in her neck.

"I'm sorry, it's just a lot for me to process. I guess I'm still not completely comfortable with this whole situation."

Chase lightly kisses the back of her neck. "You've got to chill out Jordan. Our thing is *our* thing. Nothing else can touch it."

Even though his justifications ring slightly hollow, Jordan is grateful for the attempt at soothing her nerves. "You're right," she says, relenting to the soothing touch of his hands on her skin. "Make sure you get the top right at the base of my skull. It's killing me."

The massage continues until the doorbell rings, when Chase stands to go pay for the food. He carries it into the living room and sets it on the coffee table. Jordan carefully removes the containers from the brown paper delivery sack and arranges them neatly, placing the wrapped chop sticks on top of the boxes with a flourish.

"You've always got to have it just so, don't you?" Chase laughs as he begins to tear into his food. Jordan shrugs in response and starts in on her own meal.

After a few minutes of eating in silence, Chase asks, "So what are you doing the rest of this week? Kendra," he quickly corrects himself, "I mean, I'm free until about eight tomorrow and Friday."

Jordan tries to recall her schedule. "I've got class and office hours in the afternoon on Thursday until three. Friday I have a department meeting in the morning..."

"Want to have a little 'lunch vacation' on Friday then?" he asks. "If we get hung up, I can always just duck out of work for the rest of the day."

"That sounds nice," she replies, "but I actually have plans Friday evening."

"Doing something with Darth Emmy?"

Jordan giggles. "Be nice! And as a matter of fact, the answer to your question is no. Actually, I have, well, I have a date." She offers this last bit of information casually, unsure of how he is going to respond.

Chase's head jerks up to look her straight in the eye. "What do you mean a date?"

"Well, on Monday, one of the guys at my regular poker game asked me out to dinner and to shoot pool. He's pretty nice, and I couldn't think of reason why not."

"How about because you're already seeing someone?" Chase asks angrily. "Is that a good enough reason for you?"

His reaction is so quick and intense that Jordan is caught off-guard, but she quickly regains her composure and her own eyes narrow at him.

"You're going to be the one to lecture me about exclusivity?" she blurts out, furious. "Which one of us is married here Chase? I'm afraid I don't quite follow your logic."

Seething inside, she eyes him, watching as he carefully arranges his thoughts before responding. He sighs heavily. "Look Jordan, I know I have absolutely no right to expect you to be with only me. But the very thought of sharing you, of another man touching you, it just makes me sick."

"You don't think I feel that each and every time you leave here?" she replies. "When I'm with you it seems like everything is perfect, and then you leave and I remember that you're not really mine, and you never will be. I accepted David's date because, quite frankly, I still deserve to see what else is out there."

"You're right Jordan; you are completely entitled to look, to date, to have a life outside of me. But please understand that I don't have to like it. Call it 'Only Child Syndrome' if you want. I have a hard time sharing." He tries to put an arm around her.

She shrugs off his touch, still irritated. "I'm an only child too you clown, so don't you dare play that bullshit line with me. I'm going on this date, regardless of what you think about it. If you can't deal with that, then maybe..."

"Don't even say it," he responds, kissing her quickly on the lips, and despite herself, Jordan feels herself warming to him. "You're in my life Jordan. I'm not letting you go." He kisses her again, more deeply this time, and she can feel her anger ebbing away.

She finally pulls away and looks up into his dark brown eyes. He smiles warmly and she grins in response then suddenly elbows him in the ribs.

"Besides," she responds. "It's not like I'm going to sleep with him on the very first date. Calm down, you big drama queen."

"Hey I have it on very reliable information that you are absolutely dynamite in the sack, so he'd be an idiot to not try his luck." Jordan bursts out laughing at this, and shakes her head mockingly. "I just hope that this clown treats you well, because if he doesn't, he's going to have me to deal with. On another note," he begins, "When does that roommate of yours get home anyways?"

"We have about another two hours."

"Well then, why don't we make the most of time we have?" Chase plants another kiss square on Jordan's lips, and the conversation fades away, mostly forgotten.

11 NO COMPARISON

Classic rock blares from Jordan's speakers as she pulls into a parking spot at "Gino's" a family-owned pizza joint in Atlanta. When David asked her to choose a restaurant, she selected this one because of its great food and casual atmosphere.

Ever since her conversation with Chase two days earlier, she had been apprehensive about the date. Not because David, a friend of several years from her weekly poker game, was anything other than a nice, good-looking guy, but because of Chase's fierce objection to it.

When she is completely honest with herself, she admits that this date is an attempt to put a little distance between herself and Chase. She knows that what is going on between the two of them is dangerous, not only because of his wife finding out, but because of how much she likes him.

This will be fun, she tells herself. *Just relax*. She checks her make-up in the visor mirror, gets out of the car, and heads inside.

David is already waiting at the hostess stand, a single red rose in hand. He is not any taller than her, and in her three-inch heels, she comes dangerously close to towering over him. He wears his blonde hair short, and has a neatly trimmed goatee.

While Jordan has chosen a mid-thigh cobalt blue jersey dress that always makes her feel like a rock star, accessorized with several beaded necklaces and lots of smoky eye make-up, David is the picture of 80's movie villain prep perfection, in a pink long-sleeved button down, sweater vest, neatly pressed khakis, and simple, expensive-looking dress shoes.

He smiles as she approaches, and reaches out for a quick, one-armed hug.

"You look lovely tonight," he tells her as he hands her the rose. "This is for you. I can't tell you how happy I am that you agreed to go out with me."

"Thank you David, I'm glad to be here," she says, and it's the truth. "I generally have a rule against dating guys from the game, as it can make things kind of messy if it goes wrong."

"Well, I'm glad you made an exception," he says, smiling. It looks like our table is ready," he says as the hostess leads them to their table.

It's a small square table with four chairs, and as she sits down, for a moment Jordan wonders if David is going to choose to sit next to her, or in the seat across from her. When he chooses the chair to her right, she smiles a little.

"The chair test" as she and Emmy call it, is always a way to determine how seriously a man views a date. The closer he positions himself to the woman, the more interested he is likely to be.

The two chat casually for a few minutes while perusing the menu, and when the waitress arrives, David is quick to order a bottle of red wine. "You're okay with red aren't you?" he asks her after the waitress has walked away.

"Sure," she replies, although in truth, she is not much of a wine drinker, and when she is, she only tends to drink sweet whites. Jordan quickly reassures herself that David was just trying to be gentlemanly. She really wants this night to go well, and being petty over something like drinks is not the way to do it.

"You know, the calzones here a really great," she says, trying to get the conversation going.

"Or we could just get a pie and split it," he offers. "I'm generally good with any kind of meat, onions, and peppers."

"Meat sounds good, although I usually wind up ordering the white pizza. I can't handle the onions and peppers though. You just rattled off two of my least favorite foods in the world."

"Well then, we'll skip the veggies. Besides, I don't want to have onion-breath later..." he trails off, raising one eyebrow suggestively.

That's a little presumptuous of you, Jordan thinks, although she forces herself to laugh at his remark.

Luckily, at that point the waitress returns with their wine, and David orders a medium three-meat pizza. After writing down their order, the waitress leaves, and he pours the wine. He makes a big show of sloshing the wine around in his glass, while Jordan simply lifts her glass and takes a big drink. It's incredibly dry, and she has to force herself not to grimace.

"So," he says, breaking the silence, "You're a teacher right? High school?"

"College actually. I'm a literature professor at a small university downtown."

"Well then, consider me 'hot for teacher' then," he says, laughing at his own joke.

Jordan quickly changes the subject. "What about you? You work in banking right?"

David puffs his chest out with pride. "I'm a broker. I'm the top earner at a small firm downtown. I serve mostly private investors." He continues on, talking at length about his work, the bonuses he reaps, and all of the lavish trips and meals he gets to write off as business expenses.

"Even in this economy, he declares proudly, "I'm making an absolute killing. I probably make triple your salary." He sits back and smiles, smugly.

"Probably closer to four times. Professor's don't make much, especially when you are starting out and don't have tenure." She tries to again brush his tactless comments off as a joke, but never having been a big "money" person, she finds the conversation uncomfortable.

He snorts, and replies, "I don't think I could manage that. How do you stand it?"

"Well, I love it. I have a great time getting kids to open their minds up about literature, and my students are genuinely wonderful people."

"Better you than me I guess. If a job can't keep me in the lifestyle I want, I'm out."

"Well, I guess you are lucky then, that you don't have to make that decision," she responds, her irritation finally peeking through.

"Hey, hey, don't be like that Jordan. The great thing about the life I lead, I have the ability to treat a lady right. Stick with me and I can spoil you baby." He winks, and Jordan suppresses a shudder.

At that moment, Jordan realizes that this date was a huge mistake. While David comes across as funny and likable across the poker table, in a real conversation he is nothing but boorish and crude. Chase's face, laughing at one of her jokes, flashes across her mind, and it takes everything in her power to banish the image from her thoughts, and try to carry on with the date.

A few minutes of quiet pass, during which time, David pulls out his phone, muttering "I gotta catch the score on the game," and he spends several minutes tapping on the touch screen until thankfully, the waitress arrives with their pizza.

They proceed to eat their slices in silence, and Jordan begins plotting how quickly she can escape this date from hell.

After they finish eating, David makes the mistake of snapping his fingers to get the waitress's attention and request the check, cementing his fate in Jordan's mind. When he suggests going to a bar across the street to shoot pool, Jordan swallows the last of her wine and struggles for an appropriate response.

Finally, she answers him. "Actually, I think I am probably just going to head home. I'm just exhausted from this week."

"Not having a good time?" he asks defensively.

"No, I absolutely am," she lies, hoping that she doesn't blush, giving herself away. "Classes this week have just wrecked me. Thank you for dinner."

He signs the check with a flourish and stands up to pull Jordan's chair out for her, but she pops up out of her seat before he can manage it. She picks up her purse and the rose, and smiles at him before moving for the door.

David walks her out to her car, and she offers him another quick hug, planning on sliding into her car and making her escape. However, before she can manage it, he pulls her close and plants a kiss on her mouth, his tongue and sour red wine breath invading her mouth.

She pulls away and thanks him again for dinner then gets into her car as quickly as she can. She pulls out the parking lot faster than she probably should, but she feels a deep need to put as much physical distance between herself and the date as possible.

As she drives off, she can still feel her heart pounding. She is filled with a surge of energy she doesn't really understand, so she turns up the radio to drown out her thoughts. She sings along with the 80's music that pours out her speakers, the songs of her childhood, when things were simpler.

As the power ballad ends, she knows what she really wants tonight. She pulls out her phone, finds Chase's name, and calls him up.

He picks up on the first ring. "How'd the date go?" he asks her. "Did Prince Charming sweep you off your feet?"

Jordan can't help but laugh. "Prince Charming turned out to be a total frog. I thought it was going to be a nice evening with a cool guy, but he was an absolute nightmare. I left after dinner, because I just couldn't handle it anymore."

As Chase bursts out laughing, Jordan smiles to herself. Chase DeWitt might not be the perfect guy, but she knows him so well, and knows that at heart he is a truly sweet person. He listens to her, understands her wry sense of humor, and she genuinely enjoys every moment they spend together.

His next words break her out of her reverie. "So what are your plans the rest of the night?"

"I'm going home. Emmy is visiting her family tonight, so I am just going to drink a beer and watch a bad horror movie to clear my head."

"I think I can help erase your memory. Would you like some company? A little palate cleanser perhaps?" he asks, and she can hear the slight smirk in her voice, and it makes her face flush with fondness. It takes her just a few seconds to consider his offer and make her reply.

"That sounds fantastic. I'll probably be home in about another 15 minutes," she tells him, and she can feel her heart race again, this time with excitement.

"I'm on my way," he tells her, and hangs up the phone.

Jordan tosses her phone into her purse, and once again cranks the radio, this time singing with absolute happiness.

12 THE MASK COMES OFF

"So what's your costume going to be?" Chase asks her.

Tonight is Halloween, and since Kendra is working at the Fall Festival at her school, then going out with her friends, he has decided to accompany Jordan to a party at the house of one of her poker friends.

"I'm not telling you," she answers slyly. "It's a surprise."

"Well, then I'm even more excited. I still have to figure out what I'm going to be. Are we still meeting at eight at your place?"

"Yes, but Emmy just got home, and I think she's staying in all night. Text when you get here and I will head down to your car."

"Sounds like a plan. See you in a few hours. Bye."

"Bye Chase."

He hangs up the phone, and begins to search his closet for something he can turn into a costume. Halloween has always been fun for him, as he loves the overall feeling of hedonism that comes with being someone else for a night.

Like most people who hold Halloween in reverence, for Chase, costume selection is critical. He rifles through neatly arranged hangers, his eye honed for anything that might translate. He's into the spirit more so than usual this year, because of Jordan. With her, he tells himself, he feels like he gets to be a different person.

If he was really pushed, he would admit that this is as much of the reason he is unfaithful as is his desire to have "a taste of the strange". He enjoys his life, with a comfortable job where he is respected, and a beautiful wife who keeps a picture-perfect home. Still, Chase has a need to feel excitement, to feel carefree and uninhibited, the way he does with Jordan.

Unable to find any inspiration among his regular clothes, Chase paces his bedroom, searching for inspiration. Finally, his eyes settle on the crisp, white linens of his bed.

Jackpot, he tells himself. He walks over to the chest where Kendra keeps extra sheets, removes one, and quickly drapes and knots it until he has fashioned a toga. He walks into the bathroom and eyes himself in the mirror.

"Looks like four years in the Greek system are finally paying off," he says, smirking at his reflection.

He heads down to the kitchen, where his wife has arranged their wine collection neatly on a wire rack. He selects a fizzy, sweet white, not quite a champagne but similar, and takes the corkscrew from the drawer where it is kept.

Chase takes these two items and places them on

the driver's seat of his car, and goes to play on the internet for a while before leaving.

Man it's nice to be a guy, he thinks to himself. *A woman would wind up taking much longer to get ready.* He goes to his fantasy football website, figuring that he might as well adjust his team while he waits.

***

He pulls up to Jordan's apartment complex right at eight, and shoots her a text to let her know he has arrived.

He watches her hurry down the stairs, and slowly takes in her costume. First the bright blue boots, knee-high, followed by bare thighs, then a white bodysuit with a strategic cut-out at the bust, and a red cape fastened around her shoulders. Finally, he notices the blonde bobbed wig that covers Jordan's own auburn hair.

She opens the door to the car and slides into the passenger seat.

"Wow," he breathes softly. "You look absolutely incredible Jor."

"Thanks," she grins at him. "You have the directions?" He nods. "Good, let's get the show on the road."

Chase hits the button on his navigation system to start the automatic directions, and as it calibrates, he turns to Jordan and admits, "To be perfectly honest though, I have no idea who you are. Supergirl?"

"Close but not quite. Power Girl. Supergirl is a little too much of a goody-goody for my taste," she replies, laughing.

"Is her costume always so...explicit?" Chase asks,

his eyebrows raised.

"Actually, this one is pretty tame. One of her defining design characteristics is a ridiculously, over-the-top large chest. Mine does the job just fine, but you look in the comics, and there is *way* more on display."

"Well you look ready to save the day and kick some ass. So," he says, changing the subject, "what am I in for at this party?"

"To be honest, I'm not one-hundred-percent sure. It's thrown by the guy who runs my weekly poker game, and a lot of those guys are going to be there, but there are supposed to be close to fifty people at this thing."

"Is that tool you went out with a few weeks ago going to be there?" he asks, curious just how much drama tonight is going to bring.

"David? He might, but I think everything is cool now. We played together last week and he was totally normal, so I don't think there is any bad blood."

"Good, because if he puts one foot out of line, I'll kick his ass," Chase threatens, his expression darkening.

Jordan burst out laughing. "Oh calm down..." she finds the bottle of wine on the floor, "Bacchus, I presume? The god of wine is supposed to festive and joyous. The hostility has to go dude."

Chase chuckles and admits that Jordan has a point. Their conversation is lively and teasing the entire 30 minute drive and they soon arrive at a large suburban house north of the city.

The street is lined with cars already, so they are forced to park several houses down. As they get out of the car, Chase pulls Jordan in for a kiss, whispering huskily, "I'm not sure how much I'm going to get to do that tonight."

They head inside to the party and it already in full effect. The living room has been cleared of all furniture, and over a dozen people are dancing.

Jordan takes Chase by the hand and leads him into the kitchen, which has been set up as a makeshift bar. The host, Braden, is behind a high counter, silver martini shaker in hand. He extends the other hand to high-five Jordan.

"What's shaking Peck? Glad you could make it!" Spencer's pirate costume is already in disarray, with an eye-patch turned up onto his forehead, and his white ruffled shirt already damp with what smells like beer.

"Thanks for having me Spence. This is my friend Chase." The two men shake hands, and Chase follows Jordan out onto the porch.

A small group of guys stand in a cluster, smoking cigarettes and talking loudly to one another in the way that drunks tend to do. When they see Jordan, they burst out in a chorus of her name, and take turns hugging Jordan and not-so-subtly ogling her chest.

Chase tenses up at the sight of this. After their argument a few weeks ago, he knows he has no right to get jealous of the attention Jordan gets from other men, but he can't help but be put on edge. As she introduces each of the men, Chase forgets each name, labeling them instead "Asshole Cowboy, Loser Zombie, Dorky Elf, and Creepy Gangster".

He can't help but feel possessive of Jordan. They've been friends for so long, and he cares about her so much that he doesn't want to see her with some random tool.

At least that's what he tells himself. The truth is, he simply doesn't want to see Jordan with anyone except him. While he knows this is hypocritical and wrong, it is the reality of his situation.

As time passes, the party becomes more crowded and loud, and Chase finds himself being able to lighten up and enjoy himself. When Jordan wanders off to talk to the only other girl in her regular game, he strikes up a conversation with Asshole Cowboy about college football, and finds himself having fun.

After several minutes though, he finds himself scanning the crowd, looking for her, and he heads inside to find her. As he eyes the crowd, searching for her short blonde wig, suddenly he spots her on the dance floor, dancing seductively with Loser Zombie, whose actual name, he believes, is Eli.

He strides purposefully across the living room, his long legs reaching her in only a few steps. She turns her head, sees him, and smiles teasingly as she continues to dance.

His eyes narrow and he manages to make and hold eye contact with Jordan. "May I see you outside Jordan?" he asks stonily.

Her surprise registers on her face, and she excuses herself from her dance partner, and follows Chase out into the chilly October night.

Suddenly Chase explodes. "What the hell do you think you're doing?" he asks her angrily.

"What are you talking about? I'm dancing with a friend. Relax," she tells him coolly.

"I can't believe you'd do that in front of me," he

tells her. "It's one thing for you to go on dates when I'm not around to see it, but to grind on that clown when I am right fucking here? That's bullshit Jordan."

Her expression shows her utter surprise, which only makes Chase angrier. "Are you out of your mind Chase? Did we not have this argument two weeks ago? You're married, and not to me. You are in no position to tell me who I can dance with, go on dates with, or even sleep with. You're not my boyfriend!" she yells at him.

"Well maybe I want to be!" he shouts back at her. His mouth snaps shut suddenly, and he blushes deeply, caught in a rare moment of embarrassment. "Forget I said anything. I'm sorry."

Jordan looks up at him, her eyes filling up with tears, and instantly Chase regrets his declaration.

"How is that even possible?" she asks in a breathy, small, voice.

He reaches out for her and draws her close in his arms, unable to help himself, to resist touching her. "I know it sounds absolutely insane," he tells her. "I just absolutely cannot stand the thought of anyone else with you. I want to be the only person who kisses you, who touches you. I want you to be mine."

Now it is Jordan's turn to blush. "Part of me wants that too Chase. But it's not fair to me. You're not mine, and you never will be."

Chase tilts her head up towards him and kisses her softly. "Take a little walk with me," he asks her pleadingly. "I don't want to talk about this here."

Jordan gives a small nod, allows Chase to take her by the hand, and two walk around to the front of the house and then out to the sidewalk. Behind them, the bass from the dance music at the party pulsates, making the quiet outside almost eerie.

"I don't know how to justify myself Jordan," Chase begins. "I only know that it makes me absolutely crazy to think of anyone else with you."

"I know, but you still haven't told me how this is supposed to work. I'm new to this whole thing. You're the infidelity expert..." Her joke falls flat, and the tension between them in nearly palpable.

"Please don't talk like that. I know I've done a lot of questionable things in my past, but this is different. *You* are different. In the last month and a half, I have been content in a way I never have, and it's all because of you."

"That all sounds great Chase, but can't you see how I might be a little wary?" she asks him, as a tear finally breaks free and slides down her cheek. "I can't help but think that this is all going to end with you getting bored, and me getting my heart broken."

"That will never happen Jordan," he says, trying to reassure her. "If anything, I'm nervous that I am going to be the one to get hurt," he confesses, laughing cynically. "Listen," he starts, "I don't know the magic words to make you believe in me, but I'm willing to do whatever I can until you do."

"Chase—" she begins.

He cuts her off. "Don't. Let me finish, please." He clears his throat before continuing. "I'm here for you Jordan, in any way you will have me. I know it's unconventional, and I know I am asking for an awful lot, but would you please just consider being exclusive to me? I promise I will treat you right, and do everything I can to make you happy, and never,

ever hurt you."

As he is speaking, more tears trickle down Jordan's cheeks, and she wipes them away before telling him, "I think I'd like that."

Upon hearing this, Chase scoops her up in a big hug and spins her around until she exclaims, "Stop! You're making me dizzy!"

Chase sets her gently back on the ground, making sure that she doesn't stumble in her high-heeled boots. "What do you say we head back into that party? I still haven't gotten a dance with the hottest looking superhero in the place."

Jordan grins widely, and hand-in-hand they head back into the party.

13 COMFORTABLE ROUTINE

"Looks like you're just about ready to get out of town," Chase remarks as he eyes Jordan's neatly organized suitcase sitting open on her bed.

"Just about, yeah," she replies, as she creates a stack of folders next to her bag. "I wish I didn't have to take all of these essays with me. But with finals in just over two weeks, I have got to have these graded and ready to return when the holiday is over."

"I can't believe it's going to be a week until I see you again," he admits, looking down at his feet.

"More like a week and a half," Jordan says. "It's Thursday, I leave tomorrow night, and won't be back until late Sunday. Even though my parents only live an hour outside of the city, they say it seems like I never go home anymore, so they've 'reserved' my company the entire break. I'm going to have to lock myself in my old bedroom just to get any work done," she adds laughing.

"I feel the same way. I'm getting dragged up to

Tennessee for the week with Kendra's family. It's going to be torture. Mostly because I won't be able to do this," he says, planting a quick, sweet kiss on Jordan's lips.

Today, the mention of Kendra doesn't even make Jordan flinch. Ever since Halloween they have fallen into a reliable, comfortable routine. They see each other usually twice a week, once out at Al's, their regular bar, and then at Jordan's apartment on one of the evenings when Emmy works late. Since their big fight at the Halloween party, their relationship has progressed along easily.

Chase makes plenty of time in his schedule to see, talk to, and text Jordan, and in return, she has refused any requests for dates. She tried to tell him that she doesn't really get asked out a lot, but Chase knows this to be untrue.

When they are out together, Chase often sees men looking at Jordan, and he watches how heads turn when she laughs her distinctive throaty laugh, or she tells a story about her classes, hands gesturing wildly, eyes aglow.

He has called her out repeatedly on her appeal to men, and she swears she has never gotten attention like this before. She tells him that it must be because she's taken, but Chase knows that Jordan has always been special, and that the looks she gets are the result of the fact that she now acts like she knows it as well.

Still, Chase cannot feel a sense of pride when he looks at her. Even now, Chase sees her and is taken back by how insanely lucky he is. Even luckier, when you consider that he has another woman at home and Jordan is just his "girl on the side".

"I'm going to miss you Jordan," he tells her, and it's the truth. In his relationship with her, the former wild child has found a peace he has never known with any other woman, even Kendra. He's not sure what that means for the long term, but he pushes those thoughts from his mind, determined to simply enjoy the moment.

"The entire time I am at the Barnes' I'm going to be getting dragged from family event to family event. They go full Cleaver-style: color-coordinated family portraits, mandatory game nights, and lots of conversations about when I plan to procreate, which for the record, is not for a really long time."

"That sounds...fun," Jordan replies laughing. "I'll miss you too," she adds, smiling at him. "It's going to be strange being at home. Every time I go home, my parents try to set me up with the son of one of their friends. It makes them *crazy* that I'm not married yet. I've already warned them not to try anything this week, but knowing them, they have something up their sleeve." She sighs as she goes to her dresser, removes some clothing, and arranges them neatly in the suitcase.

"You better not be going on any dates," Chase says teasingly. Last month her statement would have gotten his anxiety running, but now, he is confident of the relationship they have built, no matter how strange it might seem to an outsider. He kisses her quickly on the check, and playfully slaps her on the rear end.

"Hold it there caveman," she jokes. "I can control my own behavior, but the machinations of Thomas and Donna Peck are outside of the scope of even my powers."

"Trust me," she says, returning his slap, "anything I get roped into will be handled with polite courtesy, and I will escape as quickly as humanly possible." She grins at him. "Then I'll send you a text to torment you about it."

"You wicked, wicked woman," he cries, laughing. "Whatever am I going to do with you?"

She grins mischievously at him, and bats her eyelashes coyly. "Well?" she asks tauntingly. "What did you have in mind?"

"Well, since you're being such a bad girl, I feel like a spanking is in order," Chase replies, rubbing his palms together.

"In your dreams DeWitt," she murmurs, reaching up to wrap her arms around his neck.

They fall to the bed kissing, careful to avoid Jordan's luggage. Just as Chase is reaching to pull her shirt over her head, Jordan's phone begins to chime loudly.

"Hold that thought," she says as she reaches for the phone. "Shit it's Emmy," she says before answering. "Oh hey Emmy. You're headed home from the shelter now?" Jordan pauses while Emmy answers. "No, I don't need anything from the store. I'll see you soon dude."

Jordan hangs up the phone and turns to Chase with a pouty expression on her face. "It looks like our evening is being cut off early. Emmy is on her way."

"Damn," Chase swears. "I was so looking forward to getting you undressed one last time," he adds, winking.

"Don't worry, there will be plenty of time for that

when I get back," Jordan reassures him. "Feel free to text me at any point in the week, and I'll see you when we both get back."

"Be good pretty lady," Chase says, kissing her one last time. He wraps his arms tightly around her and hugs her once more for good measure, then makes his way for the door.

Once in the doorway, he turns around one last time and takes in the image of Jordan, beautiful even in blue jeans, t-shirt, and bare feet, then says "Bye," before letting the door shut behind him.

He takes the stairs two at a time, smiling the whole way down. Part of him is anxious to avoid Emmy, who truth be told, has always scared him a little, but the bigger part of Chase's mind figures that the faster he gets their separation started, the sooner they will be back together.

14 TENSIONS FLARE

Kendra wakes at exactly six-thirty in the morning, as she does every morning she doesn't have work. Because of how early her school starts, she is usually out of bed at five-thirty, and even after five days without school, her body is still programmed to rise early.

She slides out of bed, careful not to disturb Chase, who is snoring softly. She knows it will be nine or ten o'clock before he finally wakes up. Even after turning thirty, he still manages to sleep like a college student on his days off.

As she pulls on a fluffy white robe, she looks around her childhood bedroom, which has been meticulously maintained by her parents, a shrine to her senior year of high school, with sprinklings of college memorabilia she integrated during summer vacations home. A photograph of Kendra and her father, both beaming proudly, as she made her entrance on her school's homecoming court is pinned to a corkboard alongside photos from her first sorority formal.

She smiles as the happy memories wash over her. Her life has been a steady trajectory of successes, and while her room reminds her of the triumphs of her past, it also gives her confidence that her future is similarly bright.

Kendra pads softly downstairs, where she finds her mother Anna Barnes starting the coffee-maker.

"Coffee!" she squeals softly, "Thanks Mom, you are so on top of everything. Can I help you with anything?"

Her mother smiles kindly in response and says, "Sure, but we're not doing anything too elaborate for breakfast. Since we're going to be spending all evening prepping food for tomorrow, I figured the boys could deal with cereal or bagels for once."

Kendra laughs, recalling the elaborate morning meals her mother has provided since they arrived. "That sounds very reasonable Mom." She walks toward the pantry and begins removing clear plastic containers of cereal. She puts them on the counter and lines them up neatly. "What time do preparations begin?"

"Around one, so everyone needs to get lunch early," her mother replies, "Otherwise they are going to have to go out for lunch. We've got work to do!"

Later on today, Kendra's grandmother and her Aunt Joanne will burst into the house, arms laden with groceries, and the women will spend the next several hours preparing dishes to be served tomorrow, at Thanksgiving dinner. As much as Kendra enjoys the annual meal with her family, she also finds a deep pleasure in her family's traditional "Thanksgiving-Eve" preparations.

Kendra and Chase arrived at her family's home in Nashville, Tennessee on Saturday afternoon, and her younger brother Pierce arrived yesterday evening. When she asked her brother why he had come without his girlfriend Jessica, he tersely replied, "Things just ran their course. Can we please just move on?" shrugging his shoulders cavalierly.

Kendra suspected that Pierce's casual attitude toward his breakup was largely a front put on for Chase's benefit. Pierce has always displayed a kind of hero worship towards Chase, much to the amusement of the rest of the family. Whenever Chase was in a room, Pierce's perfect posture would slouch as to present a relaxed attitude that belied his status as an engineering student at Virginia Tech who is in close contention to be his class's valedictorian in six months.

"So will Chase be sleeping in again today Kendra?" he mother asks, snapping her out of her wandering thoughts.

"Oh most definitely. You know how he is...any excuse to get a few extra hours of shuteye," Kendra responds laughing.

"Well he'd better get that out of his system soon, don't you think? You two will be starting a family soon, don't you think?"

Kendra grabs a mug and pours herself a cup of coffee before answering. "Mom, it's before seven. Can we pretty please save the big 'life conversations' for later in the day?" She bats her large blue eyes innocently at her mother to try to offset the direct nature of her response.

Her mother looks at her strangely, before smiling and replying "Sure thing dear. I understand completely. But later I'd love to talk to both of you about it. You're not getting any younger you know, and I'm still hoping to be the 'Cool Grandma," so don't wait too long!"

Kendra rolls her eyes, but truthfully she is grateful to postpone the subject for even a little while. It seems like the question on everybody's mind is when she and Chase are going to start a family, and she's working up the nerve to have that conversation with Chase herself. She just hopes she is able to stave off the conversation with her family until she can talk to her husband first.

She and her mother chat at the kitchen table for nearly an hour, before Kendra declares that she is heading out for a run. She sneaks back upstairs stealthily and changes into her running clothes and grabs her earbuds off her dresser.

As she steps outside a gust of brisk air sweeps over her, making her grateful for the fleece pullover she grabbed at the last minute. She begins a brisk walk to warm up as she chooses a playlist from her iPod. She finally settles on a pop mix and the sounds of trendy teenybopper boy-bands that she can't help but love fills her ears.

She runs aimlessly, passing through her old neighborhood, winding through side-streets until she reaches her old elementary school. The building has no gate around the perimeter, so she heads in and runs a few laps around the track surrounding the playground.

After nearly an hour of exercise, Kendra takes a quick break, and wipes the sweat from her brow. *If only Melanie could see me now*, she laughs to herself, remembering her friend's frustration at Kendra's lack of perspiration at yoga.

Before heading home, Kendra finds herself drawn to a landmark in the schoolyard that has fascinated her since she was a child. She stands in front of a giant map of the United States, each state carefully carved out of a different color of polished stone. She remembers being a child on the playground with friends, and racing across the map, imagining she was actually able to cross the country with super-speed. Kendra smiles to herself at the memory, as she walks over to Tennessee, and, as she always does, touches her home state for luck.

As she stands, she redoes her ponytail, cranks up the volume, and takes off for home.

Upon arriving home, Kendra heads straight upstairs, notices that Chase's tossing and turning suggests he will soon be awake, and starts up the shower. She steps inside and lets the hot water run down her face and shoulders for a few minutes before lathering up with shampoo.

"Morning lady," Chase's voice calls out, groggy from being awake for only a few minutes. She cannot turn to look at him, as she is busy rinsing the shampoo from her hair, trying to avoid getting it in her eyes.

"Mind having some company?" Chase asks suggestively.

She hears him reach for the shower door, and quickly pulls it shut again.

"Not in my parent's house Chase. How many times do I have to tell you that?" she tells him irritably.

No matter how old she gets, the very idea of sex, or even a co-ed shower, in her parent's house makes her incredibly uncomfortable. A virgin until halfway through college, she prefers that her childhood home remain the symbol of innocence that it has always been.

"Fine then," Chase responds coldly. "Let me know when you're done." The bathroom door closes loudly, and Kendra can hear the rejection in his voice, and knows that she has hurt his feelings.

Still, she thinks to herself, *this is my family's home, and he needs to respect that.* She lathers her hair up with conditioner, then finishes her shower quickly, her enjoyment gone. Kendra wraps a fluffy towel around her, dries off quickly, and goes out into her bedroom to get dressed.

Chase moves quickly past her, clothes in hand, and she can hear the shower turning on as the bathroom door once again closes.

Kendra selects a pair of khaki pants and a pink, beaded, cardigan to wear, and after dressing, heads back downstairs.

***

The rest of the day passes without incident. Kendra and Chase win a game of spades against her father and brother. Eventually the tension between the two of them calms, and they begin to crack jokes with her family.

A little after one in the afternoon, her aunt and

grandmother arrive and preparations for dinner begin in earnest.

Kendra is busy mixing dough for pie crusts when Aunt Joanne looks at her pointedly and asks, "So just when exactly are you two going to be starting a family?"

Chase's head, previously buried in a book, shoots up, and he quickly replies. "Oh I think we are still a few years away from that."

Kendra's heart sinks at hearing his familiar refrain, and she shoots him a look begging him to be polite with her relatives.

"After all," Chase continues, "We're still plenty young enough, we're still working on developing our careers, and to be perfectly honest, I don't see all the fuss about having to have children anyways."

Kendra looks to her mother, aunt, and grandmother and sees her own shock written in triplicate across their faces. While Chase has put off the topic of children in the past, he has never before outright dismissed the very idea.

"I don't understand how you can even entertain the possibility of not having children. Bringing new life into the world is one of the greatest accomplishments a person can have," Kendra's grandmother responds tensely, turning to face Chase.

He raises an eyebrow arrogantly in response. "So what you're saying is that your own daughter is unaccomplished?"

"What are you talking about?" she replies. "Anna gave me two beautiful children: Pierce and *your* lovely wife" she adds, her tone frosty.

"I was talking about Joanne. She's an accomplished

career woman, but she's never had any kids. So in your book, that makes her a failure right?" Chase retorts sharply, as Joanne's face turns scarlet.

"Excuse me," Kendra's aunt interrupts, "but it appears that I have not gotten enough pumpkin filling for the pies." He voice cracks with strain as she hurries to get the words out. "I am going to go to the store and get more before the lines get too insanely long." She collects her coat and purse from where they were draped over a kitchen chair, and quickly darts outside.

Kendra's grandmother narrows her eyes at Chase critically before wordlessly resuming preparing the turkey.

Finally, Kendra breaks the silence. "Chase, can I talk to you in the living room for a second?" He shrugs his shoulders indifferently, but he follows her out into the other room.

"What the hell was that about?" she hisses at him as soon as they are alone.

"I'm just sick of everyone pouncing on us, giving up the third degree about having a damn baby," Chase tells her, the anger in his voice matching her own.

"Well you don't have to be such an incredible jerk about it," she retorts. "Aunt Joanne had three miscarriages before she and Uncle Howard finally gave up on the idea of having children, and she's always regretted it. I just can't believe you would just say such an insensitive thing!"

"Your grandmother is the one who started it," he insists petulantly. "All of that crap about how having babies is the pinnacle of human achievement...could she be any more Dark Ages?"

Kendra's eyes blaze with anger, and her voice seethes with rage as she tells Chase, "I think I have heard just about enough of your opinions today. If you aren't going to go back in there and make a sincere apology to my grandmother *and* Aunt Joanne, then I think you just need to go upstairs and butt out of my time with my family."

"That sounds fine to me," Chase replies evenly, before turning on his heel and taking the stairs two at a time.

Kendra hears her bedroom door slam shut, and she takes several deep, calming breaths before heading back into the kitchen to face her family.

15 KEEPING SECRETS

"Wake up sleepyhead!" Jordan's father has woken her up the same way for over fifteen years: a cheerful rallying cry paired with a repeated flickering of her bedroom lights.

She groans good-naturedly and sits up in bed. "Morning Dad," she mumbles. "Good to know you're still such a ray of sunshine first thing in the morning."

He laughs as he closes the door, and Jordan is left with a few moments of peace before reporting downstairs to breakfast. She looks around her former bedroom, taking in, not for the first time, how much the room has changed since she was a teenager.

Upon graduating high school and moving away to college, her parents converted her bedroom into a guest room, swapping out her black and red bed linens for a multicolored quilt and putting into storage the rich cherry furniture set Jordan had picked out in middle school and replacing it with an antique distressed dresser and wrought-iron headboard.

The only signs that a teenage girl had once lived in this room were the framed accolades that still adorned the walls. Every honor she received from kindergarten to twelfth grade was hung in a simple silver frame. Her spelling bee championship from fifth grade was nestled between her outstanding home economics student certificate from seventh grade and the first place award from the state writing fair she had earned junior year.

Jordan is the first person to admit that her parent's pride in her accomplishments has always made her feel good, but being back in this room, surrounded only by her triumphs, she feels a wave of anxiety.

Already this visit has been stilted. While Jordan is able to speak candidly about her work at the university, any mention of her personal life fills her with dread, and she quickly changes the subject. She can only imagine the reaction that her parents, happily married for nearly forty years, would have if they discovered she was having an affair with a married man. She shudders, gets out of bed, and plods downstairs in sweatpants and a faded t-shirt.

Her father has disappeared, presumably into his office to "work," his code for surfing the internet at random, and she knows her mother is probably already at the grocery store grabbing last-minute items, so for the time being, Jordan has the kitchen to herself. The turkey is in the oven, and already the distinct delicious smells of Thanksgiving are filling the house.

Jordan pours herself a cup of coffee, and takes a strawberry Pop Tart from the box she knows her mom has purchased especially for her visit, and sits at the counter, smiling contentedly. Right at this moment, without any human interaction to cloud her thoughts, she is quite content with her life.

It is only when she thinks about having to explain her relationship with Chase that her stomach turns. "No sane person would be able to understand," she mutters to the empty kitchen.

"Understand what?" her mother's voice interrupts her thoughts. Jordan, startled, turns around to see her mom, arms weighted down with shopping bags. She jumps off the kitchen stool to help with the bags.

"I was just thinking," Jordan begins, "that no one would ever understand why I don't like mashed potatoes, and make you do baked potatoes instead. Every time I mention it to one of my friends, they look at me like I'm crazy."

"Well I know your father and I feel that way," her mother laughs, setting down her bags. "I mean, who doesn't like mashed potatoes? It's practically un-American!"

"I know, I know. You guys have told me that since I was a kid. They just don't make sense to me. That texture in a warm food...ew," she adds, shuddering for effect, glad to have redirected the conversation.

"Seriously though Mom, I thought you only had a few items to buy? You've got like eight bags!"

"I just wanted to make sure we had enough food for today," her mother replies. "There's nothing worse than sitting down to Thanksgiving dinner and realizing that you don't have enough to go around!"

"It's just the three of us Mom. I'm sure there's plenty for all!" Jordan exclaims.

"Well, last night I was on the phone with Barbara Eastman, and her son Caleb came into town unexpectedly, and she and her husband hadn't really planned on doing a big meal, so I invited them to join us."

"Well that was nice of you," Jordan replies evenly, anticipating what is coming next.

"After all, holidays are a time for celebrating with family *and* friends, and the Eastman's are our regular partners for bridge, so it seemed only right to extend an invitation."

Jordan raises one eyebrow. "Uh-huh. So what aren't you telling me Mom?"

Her mother turns around, her face a mask of innocence. "Well, Caleb is a teacher himself. High school English, not college like you honey, and well, Barbara and I thought that the two of you might have some things in common and have a nice time together."

"Mom!" Jordan cries out, "You promised no match-making this time!"

"Well, it just kind of happened. And Caleb Eastman is intelligent and *very* handsome. His mother showed me a picture. What's so wrong with wanting to introduce such a nice young man to my lovely, brilliant daughter?"

"When are you going to give up on pimping me out?" Jordan replies, rolling her eyes.

"When you settle down with a nice guy sweetie, that's when. I'm glad you seem to have grown out of that 'tortured artist' phase you were in for so long," she sniffs, "but every mother just wants her child to be happy. I hate to think of you all on your own." She begins arranging items on the counter, not even bothering to look back to the child in question for a response.

Jordan rolls her eyes and sighs, knowing that there is really nothing she can say to change her mother's mind now that she has decided the matter. *Better prepare just prepare myself to survive the evening*, she thinks to herself, before walking out of the kitchen and heading back upstairs for a shower, leaving her mother to cook.

Eight hours later, Jordan finds herself seated next to a Caleb Eastman, a handsome man about five years older than she. His black hair is close-cropped, showing a hairline that has begun to recede slightly, but his light brown eyes are as warm as his ready smile.

"So what's it like teaching high school?" she asks him as the serving dishes make their way around the table.

"Probably not too different than teaching college I suspect. Some students love my class; some can barely be bothered to keep their eyes open," Caleb answers, chuckling.

"That's why I am really enjoying getting to teach upper-level classes this year. It's my first experience with anything but freshman-only courses, but the kids in there genuinely want to be there, so it keeps discussions pretty lively," Jordan says.

"That sounds great. I've always thought about teaching college, but I just can't bear the thought of more school to get that advanced degree. I guess I can empathize with my students that way."

"Well, I went for my Master's degree right out of

undergrad, and I have been accepted to a doctoral program for next fall, so I guess I'm kind of a school nerd," Jordan admits. "I put it off for a while, wanting to get some basic experience, but now I'm ready to get back into the student role."

"Do you know what you're going to focus your thesis on?" Caleb focuses on her when he asks, showing her that he is genuinely interested.

"I've been toying with a few ideas. Right now I am leaning toward 'Sexuality in Fiction,'" she tells him.

His eyebrows rise in surprise. "Really? That sounds...intense."

Jordan can feel her face flush. "It's not dirty," she stammers. "I just think that the evolution of how women's sexuality has been depicted in fiction has evolved rather dramatically over the last century, and I think, that in this country at least, it's tied to the overall liberation of the entire gender. I mean, a century ago women were depicted either as virgins, wives, or whores, and I think that there is a lot more range displayed in today's literature. I am teaching a Special Topics class on the subject this semester, and it's given me a lot of ideas."

Caleb's smile widens. "I think it sounds fascinating. When you finish your thesis, and it rocks the academic community, I will be first in line to have you sign a copy."

Jordan tries to suppress a laugh, and fails, replying "I think you'll make me the first doctoral candidate to have an autograph seeker. It's not exactly a career that tends to come with groupies!"

"I bet you could be the woman to change that. A sexy, edgy topic, written about by an intelligent, beautiful woman, I'm sure you'll get a lot of attention." Now it's Caleb's turn to be embarrassed, two spots of pink presenting themselves in his cheeks, highlighting his strong bone structure.

"Well, thank you," Jordan replies nervously, before turning her attention to the plate of food in front of her.

Suddenly an image of Chase's face flashes across her mind. She puts a forkful of turkey into her mouth, but it turns to cardboard in her mouth as she is hit with a strong pang of longing for him. She tries to eat, but she has lost her appetite.

"So, your mother said you're in town until Sunday. Do you think you might want to go to dinner tomorrow night?" Caleb asks. "I mean, I know it's kind of weird to ask about a meal at the biggest 'eating holiday' of the year, but I would love to get to spend some more time with you."

Jordan can feel her stomach lurch. "Excuse me," she says, getting up from her chair. "It's awfully warm in here. I think I need a little fresh air. I'm just going to step outside for a minute. I'll be right back."

She grabs her coat from the front closet and darts out the front door before anyone can question her. Memories of her time with Chase flood her mind: the way he smiles at everything she says, the feel of his lips, and the easy kind of history they have together, in spite of their unusual circumstances. She sits down on the front stoop, the bricks cold through her jeans.

She takes a few slow, deep breaths, and tries to calm her racing heart. She misses Chase so much it is painful. The thought of him sitting down to a family dinner with Kendra makes her feel slightly sick.

Suddenly, the front door opens. Caleb flops down on the steps next to her.

"I'm sorry if I said something inappropriate," he begins. "I just thought that we were having a great conversation and—"

"Don't worry about it," Jordan cuts him off.

"I just feel like I've upset you, and that wasn't my intention at all."

"No, that's not it at all," she says hurriedly. "It's just that I'm sort of seeing someone back home, and I am not really looking for anyone else. You seem like a really great guy, I'm just not in the market."

Caleb's face reddens. "I'm sorry. Your mother said that you were single. Otherwise I never would have asked. Does she not like your boyfriend or something?"

"Well," Jordan begins, hesitantly, "it's more like she doesn't know I have one. It's a complicated situation, and I'm not really excited to go into it with her."

"What is he married or something?" Caleb asks,

Jordan's cheeks flame and she hangs her head.

"Shiiiiiit..." he exhales dramatically. "You totally don't seem like the kind of girl who would do something like that."

"What kind of girl? A homewrecker?" she asks defensively.

"Hey, calm down," he admonishes. He sighs deeply. "I just meant that I didn't think you were the kind of person would who settle for being second on somebody's list of priorities. You sure don't need to Jordan."

"It's not like that. What we have, it's different," she

tries to explain.

"Well, what is it like then? I'm not trying to be overly critical. I just get the feeling you don't get to talk about it much. Go ahead and let it out. I haven't kept a secret from a bunch of moms since high school, so this is a nice change of pace," Caleb jokes.

Jordan begins to talk, and it's like the floodgates have opened. Her thoughts and feelings pour out freely. "We've known each other since college, and I used to have a huge thing for him, but we wound up just friends. But over the years, we've basically become each other's confidantes, and a few months ago, things changed. I know he's never been faithful to anyone for very long, but with me, I know that he's never been with anyone behind my back."

"Except his wife," Caleb counters.

"I know that, I really do. But when we are together, it's like that whole part of his life doesn't exist. It's just him and me, and things are absolutely perfect."

Jordan takes a deep breath, and continues. "I know I sound like an absolute cliché, but at this point, I feel like I have to stick with it, and see where it all goes."

Caleb shakes his head and smiles sadly. "I wish you luck with that Jordan, I really do. Just remember that there are plenty of guys out there who think you're great, and would love the chance to have you all to themselves. Don't settle for anything less than you deserve."

16 HAPPY HOLIDAYS

Jordan pops the top off a bottle of beer, and takes a deep drink. Emmy is out at a Christmas party for the shelter's staff, and Chase will be over any minute.

Jordan and Chase have only been able to spend one evening together since they got home from their Thanksgiving trips, due largely to Jordan's hectic schedule of grading final papers and providing extended office hours in anticipation of exams.

Her classes have now ended for the semester, and she is riding triumphant from the glowing course evaluations she earned this semester. Her students seemed overwhelmingly pleased by her choices in literature, her teaching methods, and the feedback she offers on assignments. Jordan feels like this bodes well for her school continuing her contract next year while she is working on her doctorate. As an adjunct professor, her future is always a little uncertain, but these reviews give her a needed boost of confidence.

She looks around her apartment, making sure that

everything is just right. She has gone ahead and cooked tonight, a rarity, and the lasagna is already setting on the kitchen counter, and a salad waits in the refrigerator.

The Christmas tree, meticulously decorated by Emmy, sits in the corner of the living room. Multicolored lights reflect off of the shiny foil paper in which Chase's gift is wrapped.

She struggled for nearly three weeks over what to give him, not wanting to give him something too "girlfriend-ish," but also wanting her gift to be meaningful an appreciated. She finally settled on a leather journal with his initials embossed in masculine block letters.

Jordan walks over to the tree, picks up Chase's gift, and fluffs the ribbons fastidiously, rearranging the strands of curly ribbon until they look store-display perfect.

"Honey, I'm home," Chase calls out, opening the front door of her apartment. She specifically left it unlocked so he could let himself in, and her heart leaps at the familiarity with which he refers to her home. While she knows it's largely ironic, she can't help but flush with pleasure at the statement.

"Merry Christmas Chase," she says, turning around to greet him. He pulls her in for a long hug, followed by an even longer kiss. "Alright you," she says, pulling away, "dinner's going to get cold, and you have a gift to unwrap."

"You didn't have to give me anything," Chase says, smiling. "I mean, you could've just been wearing a bow and that would be present enough for me."

Jordan playfully swats him, then leads him to the kitchen, where the make their plates, then sit in their usual places on the couch to eat.

"I've just got to warn you that Emmy will probably only be out for another two or three hours."

Chases twists his face into an exaggerated pout. "I thought she has her company party tonight. What gives?"

Jordan shrugs, her shoulders, used to the unusual aspects of her roommate's job. "I think it's the nature of her job. Fundraisers for her job can last for hours, but when it comes time to actually cut loose, it seems like everyone always makes it an early night. It's just not where their priorities are."

Chase exhales. "Well then, as delicious as this looks, there are more important things to take care of tonight." He places his plate on the coffee table, reaches into his coat, and pulls out a small gift wrapped in simple striped paper.

"This is for you," he says, handing it over to Jordan.

She places her own plate on the table, goes over to the tree, and retrieves Chase's gift. "I have one for you too," she says, handing him the glittery package. "Open yours first," she adds.

"This is beautiful," Chase remarks as he carefully unwraps the gift, taking care not to shred the paper. He holds the chocolate brown leather-bound book in his hands, and traces where his the letters are imprinted into the material. "Excellent! A diary in which I can record all my innermost thoughts!"

"Be quiet you smart ass," Jordan replies. "Open it," she adds nervously. "I wrote something inside."

He complies, and reads her inscription aloud, "To a truly unique individual with a gift for words." He pauses, and swallows, "Love, Jordan."

He looks into her eyes, and whispers, "Wow," then clears his throat. "This is perfect Jor. Thank you so much."

Jordan's face flushes, and she struggles for a moment, before responding. "I'm glad you like it."

"Your turn now," Chase tells her.

She can tell that the object is some kind of paperback book, and she remarks sarcastically, "A book for a literature professor? Very innovative DeWitt!"

"I think you'll like it, in spite of its utter lack of creativity," he smirks in response.

His retort piquing her interest, Jordan tears the paper without any of the caution that Chase displayed.

In her hands she holds a decades-old copy of Vladimir Nabokov's *Lolita*. "Look inside," Chase prompts.

Scrawled on the first page is Nabokov's autograph. She exhales sharply.

"Chase this is too much; this must have cost you a fortune," she tells him softly. It is an extravagant gift, but she cannot help but beam at his generosity.

"I know it was a crucial text to your first Special Topic course, so it seemed like you deserved a special edition. It's not a first printing, but—"

She leans over and kisses him deeply. "It's perfect," she tells him happily. "You're perfect. This is the coolest gift I have ever received. I can't thank you enough."

Chase smiles and says "I can think of a few ways."

He puts his arms around her and pulls her close, nuzzling her neck before kissing her again. They continue on the couch for a few minutes before his hands move towards her shirt, pulling it over her head, exposing her pink lacy bra.

"You know Jordan, I think you're pretty amazing," he mutters in between kisses on her lips, neck, and collarbone.

"I feel the same way about you Chase. I know this is all completely messed up, and probably won't last, but when I'm with you, things just feel right," she confesses nervously.

"I know just what you mean," he says, smiling. He shifts and begins placing light kisses down her stomach, and his hand reaches for the button on her jeans.

Suddenly, the front door swings open, and Emmy flies into the apartment ranting. "God, that was a bust. Whenever we try to get together socially, all we can talk about is work, which kind of kills the whole 'festive' vibe..." Emmy trails off, taking in the scene on the sofa.

"What. The. FUCK. Is going on here?" she demands angrily.

Jordan fumbles for her shirt, pulling it on inside-out.

"Emmy, let me explain," she pleads.

"Explain what? That I interrupted your little lover's night in?" Emmy's words are venomous, and Jordan winces.

"Emmy it just happened!" Jordan tries to make her understand.

Jordan watches as her roommate's eyes narrow as she looks at Chase.

He stands, chin held high. "Emmy listen, what Jordan and I do is none of your concern."

"None of my concern?" Emmy snaps. "Let me explain to you all of the ways in which this is my concern. One, Jordan is my roommate and best friend. Two, I spend all day helping wounded women heal from the endless parade of shit they have suffered at the hands of selfish asshole men. Three, you are married, you jackass, and I don't want adulterous man-whores anywhere in my world, and especially not on my fucking couch!" Tears of rage fill her eyes, and she turns to face Jordan.

"I can't believe you would sink this low Jordan. Where is your pride?"

"Shut up Emmy!" Jordan shouts. "I've listened to you bash Chase for years, and you refuse to see any of the good in him. Don't judge what you don't understand." She glares at her friend. "And this is my apartment too, so you have no right whatsoever to tell me who I can and cannot have in here. Just butt out Emmy, and mind your own damn business!"

Emmy, speechless, turns on her heel, walks into her bedroom, and slams the door.

Jordan begins to cry openly, and Chase puts a protective arm around her.

"Are you going to be okay?" he asks her worriedly. "Would you like me to stay? Maybe we can talk her down."

"There's no point. I've known her even longer than I've known you, and when she's this upset, no amount of talking is going to calm her. The best thing you can do is leave. I'll wait out the storm."

Chase shakes his head. "This isn't right. You shouldn't have to suffer through this alone."

"This was my choice as much as yours Chase, and we always knew this would be the consequence if Emmy ever found out."

"I'll call you," he begins.

"Don't," she tells him. "At least not until after the holidays. We both have a lot happening the next few weeks. Call me when you and," she swallows, "Kendra get back into town after New Year's. We'll talk more then." She wipes her eyes on the sleeve of her t-shirt, and attempts a brave smile.

"I'll be fine," she tells him before giving him a goodbye kiss on the cheek. "Merry Christmas Chase," she says for the second time, only this time it feels hollow.

His arms go around her in a bear hug. "Merry Christmas Jordan. I hope you like your book," he adds before walking out the door.

As the front door shuts, Jordan walks over to Emmy's bedroom and knocks on the door. "Emmy?" she asks hesitantly. "Can we talk, please?"

"Go to hell," is all Emmy says in response.

Jordan turns around, picks up the autographed copy of *Lolita* off the sofa, and carries it back to her bedroom. As the door shuts behind her, the tears continue to flow.

17 RIGHTEOUS INDIGNATION

I can't believe *her*, Emmy thinks to herself, glaring at her ceiling. A few minutes ago she heard "The ManWhore" leave and Jordan came to her door, begging to talk.

Emmy does not want to hear a word of anything her roommate has to say, certain that the only things she has to offer are ridiculous platitudes and self-justifications. Every day she sees women who have been used and abused by men, and she is disgusted at Jordan's actions. Any excuse she could offer up would likely only make Emmy angrier.

While many of the women she counsels at the shelter are physically abused, many more come to her psychologically wounded. The men in their lives treat them as disposable, having affairs and then leaving the women, often with children, high and dry, while they set off on new adventures with their mistresses. And now her roommate is one of *those* women. The thought turns her stomach.

More than a sense of disappointment in her choices, Emmy feels a sense of betrayal. While she and Jordan have not always seen eye-to-eye on matters, Emmy has always believed that her friend is a woman of integrity and self-respect. Now though, everything has changed, and Emmy isn't sure what to do next.

She rolls over, not caring is her usually immaculately made bed becomes a tangle of blankets, and picks up her cell. She dials the one person she can think of with whom she can talk through her twisted thoughts.

"Hello?" Her mother answers on the second ring.

"Hi Mama," Emmy says, her voice ragged.

"Emmy, why are you calling? I thought you had your holiday party tonight? You sound upset."

"Oh Mama, I don't even know where to start," Emmy admits wearily. Her mother has always been her strongest supporter, for many years she was Emmy's only supporter, after her father took off when she was just in elementary school.

"Just start at the beginning and work your way forward," her mother instructs. "I've got all evening."

"Well," she begins, "It turns out that my *best friend* isn't at all the kind of person I thought she was."

"Emmy honey, are you saying you and Jordan had a fight?" her mother asks.

"It's worse than that Mama. I came home tonight and I saw her on the couch, *topless*," Emmy spits out the word fiercely, "making out with this absolutely horrible guy we went to college with."

"Honey, your friends are allowed to date someone you don't like. That's not your call to make," her mother chides.

"No Mama, I haven't told you the worst part. He's married. Married! I feel absolutely sick to my stomach that she would even consider something so heartless and trashy."

There is a pause on the other line as her mother digests the information. Finally her mother speaks.

"I can see how that would make you upset, given what we've been through."

"You're damn right I'm upset!" Emmy retorts.

"Language Emily Jane," her mother warns.

"Sorry Mama, I'm just so angry! How could she think so little of herself, and be so horrible to his wife? She's no better than that awful woman that Dad left us for. She's destroying a family, and all she could say to me was 'I can explain.' It's disgusting!"

Emmy's anger comes from a deeply personal place. When she was in third grade, her father revealed that he had been having an affair with a woman in his office since Emmy was a toddler. Worst of all, after the revelation, he promptly moved out of the house, out of state, and into a brand-new life with his coworker. While he dutifully sent child support checks every month until she was eighteen, he has not seen, or even spoken to Emmy since then.

Over ten years ago, at the end of Emmy's second year of college, her mother received a letter explaining that her father had remarried, and had built a new family with his now-wife, including two half-brothers Emmy would likely never meet. The letter was accompanied by a five-thousand dollar check that Emmy referred to as "hush money". She used it to pay part of her tuition, and wrote her father off. She has largely blocked him from her thoughts and mentions him only when she can't avoid it.

"Emmy," her mother says softly, "Not every relationship is exactly alike. You can't judge your friend based only on your personal experiences."

"It's not just my experience Mama. It's what I see every single day at work. I don't think I will ever be able to look at her again," Emmy admits, sadness creeping into her voice. "I don't think I can do this anymore."

"Honey, don't act too rashly," her mother warns. "Why don't you come home this weekend? We can take some time, really think this all through, and make a plan to get you through this."

Emmy sighs, relenting. "Okay Mama. I'll probably be home late tomorrow though. I have something I need to take care of here first. Jordan leaves for home first thing in the morning to spend the school break with her family, so I won't have to see her."

"Now that sounds like my smart, thoughtful girl," her mother says. "I'm sure things will look less awful in the morning, and if not, we'll figure it out together."

"Just like always, right Mama?" Emmy asks, with a touch of a smile in her voice. "Thanks for listening. I'll see you tomorrow night. Good night."

"Good night honey," her mother says before the line disconnects.

Emmy sighs again, gets up, and moves over to her computer. While she knows that her mother's advice is sound, part of her is just so incredibly angry, that she knows she won't be able to let it go so easily.

She logs onto her school's alumni database, and

searches for Chase DeWitt. Social butterfly that he is, his personal contact information is of course kept up to date. She jots his information down on a sticky notepad that she keeps next to her keyboard. Emmy is not one hundred percent certain what she is going to say, but she knows that she is not going to be able to walk away from this without making sure her opinions are known.

18 SHATTERED ILLUSION

Kendra takes a step back from the kitchen counter, and takes in the spread laid out for Aubrey and Becca's joint baby shower. Finger foods are elegantly displayed on glass trays, with little containers of pink and blue toothpicks provided so that her guests don't have to dirty their hands.

She was right that her friends' request for an "intimate" shower turned out to be an affair for thirty women, only about half of whom Kendra has ever met. It is just before one in the afternoon, but Kendra has been readying the house and refreshments since seven in the morning, determined for their party to exceed even Aubrey and Becca's lofty expectations. She even sent Chase out at the "ungodly" hour of nine so that she wouldn't have to clean up after him in addition to setting up the party.

She carries the platters of food out into her living room, where folding tables are already set up, covered in pristine white tablecloths. Kendra arranges and rearranges the food until she is happy with how it is laid out. She heads back into the kitchen and one at a time carries two delicious-looking cakes, and places them center-stage on a small round table in front of the fireplace. The lemon with raspberry filling cake is frosted in white, with pastel pink accents and cursive lettering that spells out "Kayleigh" in honor of the little girl Becca is carrying, while the second is double chocolate, with "Preston" printed in careful block letters for Aubrey's soon-to-be-born son.

Ever since discovering they were having children of opposite genders, Aubrey and Becca have taken to referring to their babies as "the little lovebirds," certain that the best-friendship of their mothers will eventually lead the children down the path to matrimonial bliss.

Kendra made the mistake last week of asking "What if one of them is gay?" and the withering looks she received from both expectant mothers were enough to send chills down her spine. Still several months away from giving birth, it has become apparent that nothing about her friends' pregnancies is joke material.

Thirty minutes later, Melanie arrives to help with the last minute preparations while Kendra rushes upstairs to change. She puts on a pair of linen pants and tailored blue button-down, slides her white-gold hoops into her ears, and lightly touches up her makeup before heading back downstairs.

"You look great, as always," Melanie says, stirring the punch bowl.

"Thanks Mel," she replies. "Looks like we are ready to go. The Stepford Wives can show up any time now."

Melanie laughs. "You know most people would consider you one of them," she admonishes slyly.

Kendra shrugs.

"No, I'm serious! You have the perfect life. Great job, great guy, great looks. You've got it all."

Kendra blushes, and searches for a response. She is spared from having to provide one though, by the chime of the doorbell.

***

After the last guest has cleared out, Kendra is finally alone. She doesn't expect Chase home for another several hours, so she takes this opportunity to put her feet up and relax for a few minutes before beginning the clean-up effort. Melanie asked if she could help out, but Kendra shooed her away, just wanting to have some peace and quiet.

While her friends and sorority sisters were careful to avoid the topic of Kendra starting a family of her own, their eyes asked unspoken questions, and she is quite frankly exhausted.

All of a sudden, there is a knock at the door. Kendra looks around the living room to see if someone has left a purse behind, and seeing none walks over to the door and looks in the peephole.

Standing at her door is a woman she doesn't recognize. She is a short, slightly overweight woman with dirty blonde hair that is pulled back in a severe braid that seems to match the serious look on her face.

Kendra opens the door, and the woman begins to speak immediately. "Kendra DeWitt?" she asks, biting her lip slightly.

"Yes, that's me," Kendra answers her.

"Mrs. DeWitt, if I could just have a moment of your time…" the woman begins.

"I'm sorry, but this neighborhood is strictly 'No Soliciting,' so I am going to have to ask you to leave," Kendra replies curtly.

"No, it's not like that," the blonde replies. "My name is Emmy Trew. I went to college with your husband Chase."

"Yes?" Kendra asks, confused as to why this woman is standing at her door on a Saturday afternoon.

"I have some…information….that I really think you need to know. Could I possibly come inside for a minute?" Kendra watches the unfamiliar woman chew her lip nervously, awaiting a response.

"About Chase?" Kendra asks, unable to hide her curiosity. "I suppose so. Come on in."

Kendra does not think that this woman is any kind of a danger to her, but the serious expression on her face and her reference to Chase has made her suddenly anxious.

"Emmy is it?" she asks politely, ever the hostess. "Can I get you anything? A glass of water perhaps?"

"No," Emmy responds. "I just wanted to speak with you for a few minutes. There are some things that I think you need to be aware of concerning your husband."

"Chase?" Kendra asks, her face a canvas of confusion. "Is everything okay? Is he hurt?"

"He's fine," Emmy responds coldly. "In fact, he seems to be taking care of himself just perfectly."

"What are you talking about?"

"There's really no good way to say this," Emmy begins uneasily, chewing on her bottom lip. "Your husband is cheating on you."

Kendra's stomach lurches, and she fumbles for a reply. "You have no idea what you are talking about. Chase would never do that to me. "

"It's true," the other woman states. "I'm not sure how long it's been going on, but he is having an affair."

"You have no proof," Kendra says softly, feeling woozy. She lowers herself down onto the couch.

"I saw it with my own two eyes," Emmy explains, sitting down next to her. "The woman he's been seeing is someone he's known since college. Her name is Jordan Peck. She and I live together. I came home last night and when I came home, they were together."

"He has women friends," Kendra explains, trying to find an explanation. "That doesn't mean he was doing anything wrong. Clearly there's got to be an explanation."

"They were making out on my couch," Emmy states evenly. "I wish it weren't true. I never thought my roommate would be capable of something like this, but apparently I was wrong."

Kendra puts her head in her hands, and takes several deep breaths, trying to calm herself.

Emmy continues to talk, each work causing Kendra to wince inwardly.

"I don't know how long it has been going on, but I think it's been happening for a while." She pauses, and her eyes trace Kendra's face sadly before continuing.

"They had plates of food on the coffee table, and there was wrapping paper spread on the floor. It didn't look like any kind of a one-time thing. I can't say for sure, but it looked like it had been going on for a few months."

"But he's my *husband*," Kendra whispers, her throat tight with tears.

"I'm sorry Kendra. No woman should ever have to find out something like this, but I felt like you deserved to know."

"There has to be an explanation," Kendra says, her voice gaining strength. "I'm sure there is a perfectly reasonable explanation."

"You can ask him," Emmy replies. "I'm not in any position to tell you what to do. In my experience though, men always have 'an explanation' for the shitty things they do, and their explanations are almost always absolute garbage."

Kendra clears her throat and stands. "I think you need to go now."

"I understand that this is a lot to take in," Emmy replies. "And I know we don't know each other, but I just felt like you deserved to know what the man you married is up to when he's not at home."

Kendra watches as she stands up and walks out the front door. As the door clicks shut, Kendra looks around her living room, the remnants of the party still strewn across the room.

She walks slowly across the room and drops into a plush white armchair. It is usually her favorite place in the house to sit, but now it feels strange. Her gaze again wanders around the living room, but her house feels strange now. It no longer feels like the warm home she and Chase built together.

If this Emmy person is telling the truth, she thinks to herself, *everything we have is an absolute lie*. The thought makes her shiver, and her stomach lurches. She has to talk to Chase and get some answers.

She pulls her phone out of her pocket and sends Chase a text message, telling him to come home.

She's not sure what she is going to say when he arrives, but she knows that they have a lot to talk about, and he has a *lot* of explaining to do.

19 HOLIDAY DRAMA

Even though the magic of Santa Claus faded over twenty years ago, Jordan still wakes early every Christmas morning. She turns to look at the digital clock on the nightstand, and the familiar red digits show that it is only six in the morning. Knowing that her parents will not wake for at least another hour, she takes out her journal. Instead of writing though, today she flips back through the entries of the last few weeks and reads.

After Emmy caught her with Chase that night Jordan went to her room and cried for nearly an hour. The most frustrating thing about the situation is that she feels like she has no one to talk to about the situation. Normally Emmy or Chase is the person she turns to in times of trouble. This time however, neither seems possible. Emmy has made it clear that she wanted nothing more to do with Jordan, and Chase is not an option.

Jordan knows he is suffering too right now, both

from the impact of Emmy's fury and, she hopes, from missing her as much as she misses him. However, she can't bear to text him, is unwilling to burden him with her own loneliness.

Instead Jordan turned to her journal. She has kept one on and off since high school, and it is there that she turns when she feels she has no other outlet.

As she pours back over the pages, her face burns at the frustration and shame that she felt that night. Her anger was, and still is, largely directed at Emmy, because of her absolute refusal to listen to what Jordan had to say. Jordan knows that Emmy will never be supportive of their relationship, but it still burns to think of how her friend completely shut down.

When Jordan woke up that next morning to leave for home, Emmy's door was still shut. Not wanting to start another fight, Jordan simply hoisted her duffel bag onto her shoulder and walked out the door.

For the last four days she has pushed her stress and sadness deep down into her stomach, determined to not let the events of that night cloud her family's holiday celebration.

Lost in thought, Jordan sighs and leans back against the headboard. For a moment she had even considered asking her mother for Caleb's contact information, but she doesn't want to deal with either her mother's inquiries or the pitying look she knows she would see in Caleb's eyes at the way the situation has unfolded.

Eventually, there is a soft knock on her door, and Jordan knows that her mother has got the coffee made and it is time to head downstairs.

"I'll be downstairs in just a few minutes," she calls out, sliding her feet into a pair of fuzzy socks.

She plods down the hardwood stairs and draws a sharp breath at the sight of the tree lit with strands of tiny colorful bulbs and bedecked with the same ornaments her family has used for years. The space underneath is filled with gifts, and her family's matching stockings hang from the mantle.

Per family tradition, Christmas morning is just for stockings. The rest of the gifts will be opened later in the afternoon when her grandmother arrives.

Jordan sits down on the couch with her mother as her father passes out the stockings then settles into his armchair. They take turns opening the small gifts within, and Jordan laughs at the industrial-sized package of pens that her parents managed to wedge into the stocking.

"I figured you would need them for all of those papers you will have to grade Professor Peck," her mother explains, smirking.

"I can't imagine a more fitting gift," she says, smiling. "Maybe I should have put some Clorox wipes in your stocking Mom," she retorts before sticking her tongue out.

A small decorative pillow flies at her face in response. "Careful Mom," Jordan admonishes, "you don't want to spill this delicious coffee all over your couch!"

The stockings are emptied in short order, and soon her mother has headed off to dinner to begin the elaborate preparations for that evening's dinner of Beef Wellington, while Jordan and her father switch on the television and, after some friendly bickering, settle on the 24-hour-long marathon of the holiday classic *A Christmas Story*.

After one and half viewings, Jordan pries herself off of the couch and heads upstairs to shower before her grandmother's arrival.

Nana Peck shows up a little before one and, after her mother declares that Christmas dinner is safely in the oven, the family sits down to begin opening gifts. As the "kid" in the family, Jordan is given the first gift, and when she opens the brightly-wrapped gift, she finds a box containing an expensive designer laptop bag.

"Wow Mom, this is incredible," Jordan breathes, although the only computers she has currently are a massive desktop in her bedroom and the ancient device that sits, largely unused, in her office. Still, it is a beautiful bag, and she strokes the supple leather trim absentmindedly.

"Well, I thought that you might be able to use it, since you'll be starting your doctoral work this year," her mother responds.

"And I have something to go with it," Thomas Peck adds, picking up a large gift and placing it gently in Jordan's lap.

"No way," Jordan whispers, guessing what is inside. "This is too much you guys," she adds.

"Just open the present Brat," her father instructs, calling her by the pet name he has used since she was a teenager.

She peels off the paper carefully, and when she finally sees the laptop within, her jaw drops. "This is a top of the line piece of equipment. You guys really shouldn't have done this."

"We just wanted you to know how proud we are of everything you're accomplishing Sweetie," her mother replies, smiling widely.

"Well, I think you guys have officially topped that Barbie Dream House from second grade," Jordan jokes, her voice cracking, and tears filling her eyes. "I really can't believe this. Thank you so much."

The rest of the gift opening is fairly calm after the shock of her first two presents. Her family exchanges the usual array of DVDs and CDs, and her grandmother surprises her with a one-hundred dollar gift card for her favorite bookstore.

"Now Jordan," Nana lectures playfully, "under no circumstances are you to use that gift card to buy books for work. You have only a few more months before all you'll be able to read is required material. I want you to take some time and read for fun."

"Thanks Nana," Jordan beams, fanning herself with the gift card. "I promise you that this is officially earmarked for guilty pleasure reads only!"

After all of the gifts have been opened and the paper cleared away, the family moves to the dining room for dinner.

"Mom, this all looks and smells fantastic," Jordan remarks as she eyes the perfectly browned pastry of the Beef Wellington and the various side dishes she has prepared. "One of these days, I will need you to teach me how to make all of this stuff."

"I'd love to," her mother answers. "All you need is someone to cook for."

"Mom!" Jordan groans good-naturedly, "I thought we've been over this enough already."

"All I'm saying is that it would be a shame to

waste all this fine cuisine on a roommate who always works late. If I'm going to teach you, I'd like to know you're preparing it for someone special."

Jordan takes a deep breath and steels her nerves. She has hesitated opening up to her parents for this entire trip, and the mood is so jovial, that this probably the best shot she's going to get.

"Actually Mom, there's someone I've been seeing recently."

Three shocked faces turn towards her then her mother shakes her head and regains her composure, as her father and Nana look on.

"That's wonderful honey!" her mother replies. "Why didn't you tell us earlier?"

"We can talk about it more after dinner," Jordan says, a feeling of nervousness building in the pit of her stomach

"Nonsense," her mother replies. "Your father can serve the meal as you tell us all about your new boyfriend."

"Well, he's not exactly my boyfriend Mom. It's kind of complicated," Jordan begins.

"Your generation, you fuss so much over labels," her mother sniffs in response. "It's just so silly. If he's a man and you've been seeing him, he's your boyfriend."

"It's not as easy as that," Jordan tries to explain, but her mother just rolls her eyes, while the other members of her family watch, riveted.

"His name is Chase, we've known each other for a really long time, and it's just in the last few months that things have taken this kind of a turn."

"Chase..." her mother begins. "I remember a

Chase from college. This wouldn't be the same boy? The one that broke your heart so badly back in school?"

Jordan forces a laugh, "Funny enough Mom, it's the same guy. Things have changed a lot since then, and it just felt like the time was right for us. It's been kind of difficult though, because Emmy doesn't approve, so things have been a little tense around the apartment."

"Well what give Emmy the right to have an opinion in who you see?" her mother asks.

"That's exactly what I was thinking," Jordan answers. "It's not her life, but she insists on telling me how to live it. We had a bit of a fight before I came home, and I'm not sure what I'll be walking into when I go home at the end of the week."

"Well what's her big objection? He's not one of those 'potheads' is he?" her father interjects.

"Oh no, nothing like that," Jordan answers. "It's a little more complicated than that."

"Well then what is it?" Nana Peck asks her.

"He's married," Jordan mumbles.

"What? I don't think I heard you properly" her mother responds.

"He's married," Jordan says, a little louder this time. She looks up and sees the disapproving faces she has dreaded for months.

"Please don't," she says as her mother opens her mouth to speak. "I don't want to go into it. There's more to it that I am not discussing right now. Just please understand that he makes me happy."

Her mother closes her mouth, and the family hesitantly begins their dinner. The meal is delicious, but Jordan barely tastes a thing, desperate to finish her food so she can remove herself from this situation.

She excuses herself to her room as quickly as she can, and spends the rest of the day reading and venting into her journal. No one comes up to speak to her, and she eventually falls asleep early.

***

The next few days pass slowly and painfully, until finally it is time for Jordan to head home. The miles pass quickly, the pine trees lining the highway a blur of color, as if her car can feel her desperate need to be home.

She unlocks the door to her apartment, and opens the door to a half-empty living room. All of Emmy's belongings are gone.

Jordan walks from the living room into Emmy's bedroom, and finds it equally empty. She wanders back into the kitchen and eventually finds a note on the counter.

Jordan-

I can't live with a person whose values so clearly clash with my own. I've left a check for the next month's rent, but I can't be here anymore.

-Emmy

While her words hurt, in a way Jordan is relieved to have some of the tension in her life gone. The apartment may be missing a lot of furniture, but at least she no longer has to worry about feeling like her every decision will be judged.

Jordan keeps herself occupied that evening by preparing her syllabus for the spring semester, and trying to avoid thinking about Chase and when she will hear from him again.

Finally, on New Year's Eve, Jordan looks through her DVD collection and selects a variety of horror movies. For years she has avoided the expense and drama that New Year's seems to unavoidably bring, instead opting to watch teenagers get horribly slaughtered on her small but crisp flat screen television.

As she loads up the first movie into the player, she hears a knock at the door. Thinking it might be Emmy back to retrieve some forgotten object, she makes her way hesitantly to the door and peers through the peephole.

When she sees Chase, she flings the door open with excitement. As he stands solemnly in her doorway thought, she knows that something serious has happened. His cheerful grin is nowhere to be found, and a satchel is thrown over one shoulder. He throws his arms around her though, and holds her tight for what feels like an eternity.

Jordan can feel a difference in the way he holds her, and she knows something has changed. Though she is unsure what this means, for now she is just content to be held by the man she loves.

20 CLEARING THE AIR

Slowly, over the course of a several hours, the entire story comes out. Jordan sits on the couch, listening with rapt attention as he describes to her how it all happened.

***

He got a text from Kendra telling him to come home. Before he had even walked in the door that day, Chase knew something had gone wrong. Kendra was standing in the doorway when he pulled into the garage, her arms crossed and eyes stormy.

"Who's Jordan Peck?" she demanded before he had even closed his car door.

Chase had just paused, dumbstruck, trying to figure out a response, to guess exactly what Kendra knew.

Part of him had always known that this day could one day come, when his actions would be discovered and he would have to account for himself. Still, he had never prepared for it, because he was so certain that he would never be caught. Looking at Kendra though, he knew that his confidence, his arrogance, was about to become his downfall.

"She's a girl I went to college with," he answers, his voice free of any waver.

Kendra's eyes narrowed, and when she spoke again, it was in a tone he had never heard from her before. "So what you're saying to me Chase, is that she's *not* the woman you been sleeping behind my back?"

"Kendra, let me explain," he started to say, before she cut him off.

"Explain what? That you're a cheating, lying bastard? How about you explain this: how long has this been going on?" Her tone was frosty and imperious, but the tears that were welling up in her eyes had shown Chase how deeply he had hurt his wife. He paused, fumbling for a response that might alleviate some of that paint.

"It's been going on for about three months," he admitted, figuring that there was no point in hiding anything anymore. He had thought for a moment that honesty could maybe make everything okay.

Kendra blinked, and the tears began falling freely. Her shoulders slumped, and she seemed instantly drained of energy. "So was it just this one woman, or have there been others?" she asked in a small voice.

"Kendra..." he sighed.

Though he had thought she would have turned on him in rage, the truth had seemed to leave her defeated. Finally, she had drawn a long slow breath, and told him in a chillingly calm voice:

"Don't even bother Chase. I have no interest in what you have to say. All that matters is that you're a cheater, and I refuse to have anything to do with a man like that."

Chase had been unable to come up with any kind of response, so he had simply nodded before putting his head in his hands.

"I'm leaving now for my parents' house. I will be there until the 28th. I don't know what exactly I will be doing next, but I do know that by then I want you out of this house."

Chase had opened his mouth to argue, as the house belonged to both of them, and they both contributed equally to its upkeep. Before he could say a word, Kendra had again cut him off.

"I don't care about details right now. I just know that I can't look at you, and I would be perfectly happy to never see your face again."

With that, she had walked past him, got in to her car, and drove off, leaving him alone in the house that was a shrine to the life they had made together. That life, he knew, was now destroyed, and Chase had to admit he had only himself to blame.

The next few days had passed in a fog. Chase knew Kendra well enough to recognize that she had meant every word she said. He spent Christmas Day packing up his belongings into suitcases and boxes, eating that same cold pizza that had fueled him the two days prior.

He had even moved several of the boxes he didn't need immediately into his office, for fear of what might happen if he left them in the house unattended. He felt a little silly, but still gave in to his paranoia.

When the 28th rolled around, Chase checked into the Atlanta Westin. He had known that Kendra would probably leave town the next day for her trip with her friends, but he didn't want to chance running into her, so he had stayed there ever since. However, the luxurious hotel did little to quiet his racing thoughts.

Finally tonight, on New Year's Eve, he got in car and had driven over to Jordan's apartment. He walked the steps to her apartment not knowing what he would find. He prayed Emmy wouldn't be home, not wanting to get into it with her again. More than that though, he was afraid that Jordan wouldn't want to see him, that she had decided to adhere to her roommate's advice and shut him out her life.

***

"I almost called you a hundred times Jordan," he tells her. "But I stopped myself because I didn't want you to think I was just leaning on you because I screwed up my own life."

"You didn't have to do that," she whispers in response. "You could have called me."

"No, I couldn't. I needed to take time for myself, and sort through my own thoughts. Finally though, I realized that I didn't just want to see you. I *needed* to see you."

Jordan's eyes go wide at the intensity in his voice, and sensing he has more to say, remains silent. Her nerves are on edge with the anticipation.

"The truth is Jordan, being with you these last few months has made me happier than I've been in a really long time. Happier than maybe I ever was with

143

Kendra."

She blushes, but lets him continue.

"The fact of the matter is that you've become more than a friend, more than someone I'm attracted to. You've become the most important person in my life."

Jordan is still speechless as she watches him reach into his bag and pull out the leather bound book she gave him for Christmas. He opens the cover and looks at the inscription.

"You wrote something very specific in this book. Did you mean it?" he asks her, his dark brown eyes searching her face for a reaction.

"Chase, I am so ashamed of you," she tells him, and his face falls.

"I'm ashamed that you even need to ask such a stupid question," she continues as her face breaks out in an enormous smile.

Suddenly, for Chase, the room seems brighter, the green in Jordan's eyes more vivid. His smile is all the response she needs.

"I love you Jordan Peck," he tells her, taking her hands in his.

"I love you too Chase," she murmurs back as he pulls her close in a hug.

They stay like that for several minutes, her face buried into his neck, inhaling the sharp smell of his aftershave, as he strokes her short auburn hair, marveling, not for the first time, at how soft it feels against his fingers. Finally, he feels her turn her head, and when he looks down he can see her gazing up at him.

"I have an idea," she tells him, leaning back.

"Clearly I no longer have a roommate," she says, gesturing to the half empty apartment, "and I really can't handle the rent on this place on my own. What would you think about taking the spare room?"

Chase smiles in spite of his surprise. When he came over tonight, all he wanted was to see Jordan and tell her how he feels. This development is more than he ever hoped for.

Jordan continues, "I'm not suggesting that we share a room, or that things are more than they were two weeks ago. However, I have a room, you need a place to stay, and I think that right now, we need each other. What do you say we just give it a try for a month or two?"

"I think that is a perfect idea," he replies.

All of a sudden, cheers erupt from the porch of the apartment next door, creating a roar that shatters the quiet solemnity of the apartment. Jordan's eyes dart to the clock.

"I guess that means it's now midnight," she says, standing and stretching. "Happy New Year Chase," she tells him, smiling.

He rises to join her, and pulls her close into a soft kiss, different from any they have shared before. It is gentler, more careful, and feels almost hopeful.

"Happy New Year Jordan," he responds. "Despite everything, I think it just might be a great one for us. Who knows? Maybe this was just the way that things were supposed to play out."

"Maybe," she answers. "I'm just glad to be starting this year here, with you. I can't imagine being anywhere else tonight."

"Me neither," Chase responds, before pulling her

in for another kiss.

Outside the apartment someone is shooting off illegal fireworks, and the bang and crackle of the colorful explosions fill the air for close to an hour. However, they are so consumed with one another that neither Chase nor Jordan notice. For now, this apartment, now their apartment, is the entire world.

21 ABSOLUTELY PERFECT

It is the Saturday before Valentine's Day, and Chase feels like his life is looking up. The last month and half of his life haven't always been easy, but things seem to be clicking together.

On New Year's Day, he and Jordan moved his belongings into the apartment. He set up a futon in the second bedroom, but the idea of sleeping in separate rooms was discarded on the first night.

Over the last few weeks, he and Jordan have settled into a comfortable routine. They both go to work, and once a week she has her regular poker game. However, most nights they wind up at home, relishing their newfound ability to be together without fear, without anxiety. It feels peaceful and warm, and Chase feels a sense of calm and ease he has never felt in a relationship before. It feels nice, like something he never knew he'd been missing.

The one rough spot for him has of course been Kendra. About a month ago she called him and informed him that she was in the process of filing for divorce. For a moment he thought about trying to convince her to change her mind, but he knew that no amount of persuasion would change her mind.

The papers arrived at his office yesterday. Chase guessed that since she hasn't asked where he was living, she had truly written him off.

He is recalling these events as he walks into the restaurant to meet Greg. He had told his big brother about the split via text message, and nearly instantly found himself on the receiving end of a scathing phone call. Greg had demanded that Chase sit down with him in person, so they had decided on a local pub where they have gotten together for beers on several occasions. Chase feels more comfortable at Al's, but since that is the bar he frequents with Jordan, he wants to keep today's meeting on more neutral territory.

Chase spots Greg the instant he walks in. He is sitting in a side booth, and the look on his face tells Chase that he is in for something more painful than anything dished out during Initiation Week.

He sits down across from Greg and smiles weakly. "How's it going bro?" he asks casually, hoping to avoid a lecture.

"Well, I'm missing my kids' basketball game because you've made such a mess of your life that someone has got to straighten your ass out. How do you think I'm feeling?"

The sarcastic, judgmental tone in his voice immediately puts Chase on the defensive. "So I don't get a chance to defend or explain myself?" he demands angrily.

"If you think you've got anything worth saying," Greg shrugs in response.

"I tried to talk to you about this months ago! You shut me down without listening to a thing I said. So don't just immediately jump on my case. I agreed to meet you today because we are friends, and I could use one of those right now."

Greg is quiet for a moment. "I guess I can see where you are coming from. I'll suspend the lecture long enough to let you explain what the hell happened. But if you're as big an idiot as I think you are, I reserve the right to pick up right where I left off," he replies.

At that point a waitress comes buy and takes their drink orders. Despite the fact that it is only two in the afternoon, both men order beers. Silence lingers for a few minutes after their drink order is taken, until finally Chase speaks.

"Do you remember Jordan Peck?" he begins.

"Jordan, Jordan...was she that flight attendant you were nailing in your mid-twenties?"

"No!" he answers quickly. "She went to school with us. Reddish-brown hair, short, green eyes...Lit major, freaky smart?"

Greg's eyes flash with recognition. "Oh yeah, I remember her." He pauses then asks, "Wait, she's the girl you were talking about?"

Chase smiles in spite of himself, picturing Jordan's smile, imagining the feel of her body in his arms. "Yeah, well, about a week after we talked, things started happening. I hate to sound like a girl here, but I've had a thing for her for years. Since college really, and I just never got over it I suppose."

"So what stopped you before? Why wait until you were married man?"

"It always seemed like the timing was wrong. I knew back in college that I was having way too much fun sleeping around to give it up, and I couldn't stand the idea of hurting her. She's a great girl Greg. You'd really like her."

"That's probably true, but do you realize that what you've done is hurt the woman you promised to take care of for the rest of your life?" Greg's tone is light, but the question stings.

Chase inhales, and chooses his next words carefully. "I know that, I do. With Jordan though, everything is just easy, and it made me think, why aren't things like that with Kendra?" He shakes his head and admits "I don't think she and I should have ever gotten married. We just weren't right for each other."

"What are you talking about? You guys always seemed so great together."

"Well, to start, the kid issue came up a lot. I don't know if I ever want kids, and it was clearly on her schedule. When we got married I figured I would eventually get there, but it just didn't happen."

He pauses there, and Greg waits quietly for Chase to collect his thoughts.

After a moment, he continues. "Eventually, Jordan and I got caught, and the person who found out went ahead and told Kendra. So, now she's decided she wants a divorce, and I've decided the best thing to do is to just accept it. So I've moved out, and the papers arrived earlier this week."

Greg lets out a whistle. "You've been through a lot

dude. I'm not going to say that you're not an idiot and that your actions are excusable, because you are ant they definitely aren't. However, at least you seem to be getting a little smarter about it now."

"Yeah," Chase answers. "I'm trying to be better."

"So where are you living now?" he asks.

"Well, that's kind of funny," Chase begins.

"Oh god," Greg groans.

"The girl who caught us was Jordan's roommate, and she moved out of their apartment right around the time she told Kendra everything. Long story short, Kendra threw me out, so I needed a place to stay, and Jordan was in need of someone to help with the rent. So, I'm in the other bedroom."

The look on Greg's face tells Chase that any sympathy he has garnered today has just evaporated with this statement.

"Have you completely lost your mind?" Greg demands.

Chase half expected that this would be Greg's reaction, so he simply shrugs, and replies, "Maybe. It just seemed like the most logical solution. We have separate bedrooms, so it's not like we're totally shacked up."

"Bullshit DeWitt," Greg counters. "Answer this for me. How many nights a week do you two share a bed?"

Chase feels his face flush, and dodges the question. "I really just need some support on this dude. Jordan is really important to me, and I know I acted like a total jackass to Kendra—"

"That's for sure."

"Just listen," Chase says. "You don't have to like

everything I'm telling you, but just listen. I don't know how all of this is going to work out, but right now, this feels like the right thing."

Greg sighs heavily. "All right man. I'm going to refrain from judgment just yet. Just not too many details, please. I can't deal with a play-by-play of your escapades."

"You've got a deal."

The two finish their beers in relative quiet, only occasionally commenting on the basketball game playing on the big screen in the bar. After their checks are dropped off, Chase pulls out a few bills and lays them on the table.

"I've got to jet Greg. I have a few more things that I need to get done before I head back. See you later."

"Take care Chase," Greg replies as Chase walks away.

Chase walks out to his car, gets in, and smiles. While the conversation could have gone a lot better, it could have also been much worse, and he feels like he has gotten Greg to at least look at the situation from his perspective.

He pulls out of the parking space and heads down the street to the mall. He wants to pick out a really special gift for Jordan for Valentine's Day. With Kendra, it was always incredibly simple. Flowers sent to her work, dinner at whatever trendy restaurant she was excited about that week, and charm for the bracelet he gave her for their first anniversary. Jordan is much more difficult, because although they have been friends for years, this is the first time they will be celebrating this holiday, as it is generally reserved for couples.

He finds a space not too far from the main entrance, and heads inside. He walks past a make-your-own stuffed animal store that seems too cutesy for someone as edgy as Jordan. He finally heads into a jewelry store, figuring that while it is a slightly cliché choice, it would be a good starting point.

Chase stands in front of a wide, brightly-lit glass counter, overwhelmed at the array of necklaces, earrings, bracelets, and rings that glitter under the fluorescents.

"May I help you?" an older woman asks. Chase looks at her name tag, which reads "Dawn".

"That would be great Dawn. I'm looking for a gift for my," he pauses for a moment, looking for the right word. "Girlfriend," he finishes decisively.

"Ooh, you look nervous," she teases gently. "First Valentine's Day together? I can always spot a first-timer."

"Yeah," Chase admits, grinning sheepishly. "But I've known her for a really long time, so I want to get her something she'll love."

"Isn't that sweet!" Dawn replies. She walks over to the end of one counter. "Over here we have our charm bracelets. They are great for new relationships, because it is something you can build on throughout your time together."

"No!" Chase exclaims. "I mean, no thank you," he says more calmly. "I think I want to go a little more 'wow' for this girl."

"I can see your point. Well, what kinds of things is she into? That can often give me ideas of what I can recommend."

Chase pauses to think. "Well she's literature

professor, and she's starting her doctorate this fall."

"Well we have a lovely pair of sterling silver earrings in the shape of books," Dawn suggests.

"I don't think so. I don't think that's really her style. The only earrings she ever wears are studs or hoops. Really basic stuff."

Dawn eyes him, and says, "She doesn't seem like much a jewelry girl, does she?"

"No," Chase admits.

"Well, this is probably bad business for me to say, but what are you doing here then?" Dawn asks.

"I don't know. I guess I just want to make this Valentine's Day really special for her."

"What does she do when she's not at work?"

"She likes to read. We watch TV. Normal stuff," Chase replies slowly. "She plays in a weekly poker game though. She's nuts about Texas Hold 'Em. She even makes me change the channel from football to watch the World Series of Poker on television," he says, when inspiration suddenly hits him.

"I've got it!" he grins, and Dawn the saleswoman smiles cheerfully.

"Well then good luck young man," she tells him. "I'm sure that someone as thoughtful and sweet as you will come up with the perfect idea.

"Thank you," he tells her before walking away. He walks back out into the mall, mind racing, planning. He bypasses all the stores, knowing that none of them will hold the perfect gift for Jordan. In order to get her the perfect gift, he's going to need his computer and make a few phone calls to make sure everything is absolutely perfect.

22 THE DUST SETTLES

Kendra spots Melanie the instant she walks into the wine bar they always go to with "the girls". Tonight though, it is just the two of them, as all of the other girls are out with their husbands.

It is difficult for Kendra to think of herself as a "single girl" after so many years with Chase. Still, she knows that leaving him was her only option, as she has always told herself she would never stay with a cheater.

Still, seeing all of the red and white streamers draped around the bar, and the couples leaning towards one another, having intimate conversations over wine, fills her with a pang of longing for her old life, before she found out about Chase. Last year, they would have been one of those couples.

Kendra is not a woman who changes her mind easily though, and their divorce papers have already been signed by both parties, and they are simply awaiting a court date. They were able to agree on the division of assets easily, as Kendra is not pursuing spousal support, and Chase really only wanted an equal share of the sale of their home and the contents of their checking and savings accounts. Part of her thinks that his acquiescence is the result of his guilt, but she quickly tells herself that if this has to happen, if she has to endure the pain and embarrassment of a divorce, at least it is happening as easily as possible.

For indeed, the last two months have been humiliating for a woman as goal-oriented as Kendra. Admitting that she chose poorly in selecting a husband, that her "perfect" marriage was really the farthest thing from ideal, have taken a toll on her overall confidence.

"Hey Melanie," Kendra greets her friend, sliding down onto the plush leather couch next to her.

"Hey honey," Melanie replies. "I won't ask how you're doing, because I know you must feel like hell right now."

"That's putting it lightly," Kendra admits. "There are times I wonder if I've made the right choice."

"You're better off without him," Melanie tells her. "You know what they say: 'once a cheater, always a cheater'."

"I know, I know," Kendra says. "I could never trust him again anyways. I mean, who's to say this was even the first time he's done something like this? I can't be the kind of woman who lets a man walk all over her."

"Absolutely," Melanie agrees loyally. "So it looks like this is going to be over in the next few weeks?"

"It really does," Kendra says. "Although I think it's going to take me a while to really process everything.

I think I'm looking at a long stretch as a single woman."

"Can't say I blame you," Melanie replies. "At least you've got friends to support you through this."

"This is true," Kendra says, thinking about how wonderful her friends were immediately following the discovery of Chase's infidelity. After throwing him out of the house, she went home for a few days, and spent most of Christmas crying into her family's collective shoulder.

Once she came back to Atlanta though, she was determined to be strong, and that was when her girls really stepped up. They all came to the house the night she got home, and informed her that not only were they all still taking their trip to Panama City Beach together, but that all their husbands would be left at home.

Kendra smiles at the memory of that trip. They laughed and danced and walked on the beach even though it was insanely cold, daring each other to dip their toes in the Gulf of Mexico. Instead of clubbing and expensive dinners, as was the norm for these trips, they ordered in pizza and all of the non-pregnant girls got pleasantly drunk on deliciously dry white wine for three nights straight.

On New Year's Eve, she stood on the beach, crunching the sand between her toes, staring up at the stars. At that moment, she made a promise to herself that she would be strong through whatever came next, and so far, she's kept the promise admirably.

"It's just really hard," she tells Melanie. "I just never thought that I would be in this situation again. Starting all over, you know?"

"No one goes into marriage expecting to get divorced," Melanie replies. "But you also didn't think you had married a cheater," she adds.

"You're right," Kendra admits. "His choices created this situation. None of it is my fault." Her voice becomes strained, and tears well up in her eyes. "It's just so damn hard," she says.

Melanie hands her a napkin, and tries to reassure her. "I know it is Kendra. But you're strong, and you'll come out of this just fine. I know it."

Kendra smiles weakly, and leans into her friend for a hug. "Thank you. I needed to hear that."

"Anytime," Melanie tells her. "Now I think the solution for this situation is more wine!" She raises a hand to catch the server's eye, and within minutes, new glasses are in their hands.

"Let's focus on the positive here Kendra," Melanie says after taking a large sip from her glass. "Just take a minute and think about every little thing about that jerk that ever got on your nerves," she says, carefully avoiding Chase's name, "and tell me all about it. I mean *anything*."

"Well, it is kind of nice to not be subjected to his smelly workout clothes anymore," Kendra begins.

"Good, go on."

She thinks for a moment. "And I absolutely hated it when he came home reeking of pot. He swears he hasn't done it in years, but anytime he goes out with his old frat buddies, it's all over his clothes. I never really believed that he just sat around while they all got high."

Melanie smiles and nods for Kendra to continue.

"Chase was utterly incapable of putting the seat

down. I mean *ever*. Do you know how many times I wound up with a wet rear end in the middle of the night because that man can't lower a piece of plastic?" Kendra giggles, knowing that this is petty and ridiculous. In this moment though, petty and ridiculous is just what the doctor ordered.

Her best friend reaches out for her hand and gives it a tight squeeze. "I'm here for you, no matter what," Melanie tells her.

"I'm really glad I have someone like you I can talk to," Kendra says. "You always know how to make me feel better."

"What are friends for?" Melanie replies, embracing her in another hug. "So what's your plan from here?" she asks. "Going to dye your hair black and go all 'emo' on me?"

Kendra bursts out laughing in spite of herself. "I don't think so," she retorts. "Do you have any idea how few women have hair this naturally blonde? I'm not going to risk messing that up!"

"That's my girl," Melanie grins.

"Really though, I'm not sure what's next for me. I want to stay in the area, because I love my job. I will probably try to find a place closer to my school. Take more yoga classes."

"Sounds good to me."

"Who knows? This summer I might even try to travel a little bit. Go to Europe and visit the art museums I've always wanted to see." Kendra smiles, and straightens up, feeling her old confidence wash over her, even if only for a few minutes. "Who knows? Maybe I'll even do it backpack-style. Stay in hostels for next to nothing. Have an adventure."

"I think that could be just what you need," Melanie says. "Get out there and do something you never thought you'd be able to do. Trust me," she adds, smiling at Kendra. "Being single at twenty-seven really isn't so bad. I may whine about it from time to time, but it is kind of nice to have no one to answer to."

Kendra pauses, thinking. "You're right. Chase has spent who knows how long being a selfish jerk; doing whatever the heck he wanted. Now it's my time."

23 UNEXPECTED NEWS

Jordan unlocks the little metal mailbox assigned to her apartment, and pulls out a thick envelope. The return address is the doctoral program she has been accepted into, so she flips it over and quickly runs a fingernail along the seal, opening it. She pulls the paper out and scans the top page.

"Yes!" she exclaims, unable to keep her happiness to herself. Her program has agreed to accept some of the classes she will be teaching at the university in the fall as part of the teaching assistant requirement. She will still have to T.A. for one class, keep up her current responsibilities at work, and manage a full-time student schedule, but Jordan is relieved she will be able to keep her source of income. It will be incredibly busy, but she is confident she can manage it.

She pulls out her cell phone to send a quick text to Chase, and heads up the stairs to the apartment. *Their* apartment, she now thinks of it.

The last two months have been some of the happiest of Jordan's life. Life with Chase DeWitt has exceeded her hopes. She loves the consistent routine they have fallen into, from once weekly evenings of Chinese takeout and television, to the frequent nights that she spends stretched out on the sofa grading papers as he reclines back in his easy chair.

The fevered desire that fueled their first few months together has calmed somewhat, although she still feels a rush when she looks at him, and her stomach leaps when Chase wraps his arms around her. Overall though, they have a comfortable familiarity that stems from the many years of friendship they have shared.

***

However, Chase is still able to surprise her with his sentimental side. Three weeks ago, on Valentine's Day, he showed up at her office after her final class of the day bearing flowers, and drove her back to the apartment, despite her protests that they would just have to return to get her car later.

When they arrived at home, Chase told her to close her eyes before he opened the door. She did so hesitantly, but when she was given permission to look, she was stunned to see a poker table laid out over their small kitchenette table. A fresh deck of cards was spread neatly across the green felt, and multicolored poker chips spelled out "VEGAS" in bold block letters.

"Are we reenacting our first night together?" she joked, genuinely unsure of what he had in store.

"Not quite," Chase grins, "but I'd be happy to play

strip poker with you any time you like."

She stuck her tongue out at him in response, asking, "No seriously, what is all of this?"

"It's your Valentine's day gift," he told her. "At least, it's the start of it. Unfortunately I can't give you the rest for another month."

"What are you talking about?" Jordan had asked him.

"I booked us tickets to Las Vegas for your Spring Break!" he told her excitedly. "We're going to stay in the Bellagio, do a little gambling, and take in a few shows."

Jordan remembers how her jaw had dropped when he told her. "Are you serious?" she had asked.

"Absolutely," he replied. "I know that you don't really get to travel often, and I want you to have a proper vacation. I'm pulling out all the stops Jordan. It's going to be amazing."

"It sounds like it," she breathed excitedly. "This is too much though," she had tried to explain. "First the book, now the trip…"

"Don't worry about it," he told her. "As far as I'm concerned, I've missed out on years' worth of special occasions, so I'm making up for it now."

Jordan had flushed with embarrassment at his generosity, but had finally accepted his gift. They had celebrated the holiday with dinner and drinks at home, followed by a game of poker for "old time's sake".

***

Now, weeks later, the trip is less than a week away and Jordan is a mixture of excitement and nervousness. She has never gone on a trip with a significant other before, and even though they live together, she is anxious to see how it turns out.

Always one to be organized, she decides that this is a perfect time to do an inventory of her wardrobe and make sure she has the proper clothes for the trip. The tail end of winter is still present in Georgia, but in Las Vegas temperatures are already in the eighties, so she pulls the plastic bins that hold her summer clothes out from under her bed.

She neatly searches through the bins, selecting a variety of capris, shorts, and skirts as well as tank tops and short-sleeved shirts. She lays them out on her bed, swapping pieces around until she has a variety of outfits on display.

Not too bad, she thinks to herself, before remembering that Chase plans to take her to several upscale restaurants and clubs, so she delves into the bins again until she has found three appropriate-looking sundresses.

Knowing that none of these clothes will be of use before the trip, she pulls out her large suitcase. This will be the first time Jordan has actually used it, as the only traveling she has done in the several years since its purchase is to go home for brief visits. She unzips and opens the bag, and begins to carefully arrange the garments.

She examines her handiwork and smiling to herself, grabs a pen and a sticky-note pad from her desk and begins making a list of all the things she will need to add at the last minute. She writes down "toiletries, underwear, shoes," and is about to add "sandals," when her phone rings.

Glancing at the screen, she sees it is her mother, and after a moment's pause, she answers.

"Hello?" she says hesitantly, for conversations with her family members has been awkward since her declaration on Christmas. Her mother made it very clear that she disapproved of Jordan's relationship with Chase and even news of his separation was unable to change her perspective.

"How are you honey?" her mother asks.

"Things are actually going pretty great," Jordan answers, for it is true: at this point, she cannot imagine her life going any better. "I got my confirmation letter today that I can use my teaching position as some of my doctoral responsibilities in the fall, so I'll be able to keep my position while I'm in school!"

"That's wonderful!" her mother responds, genuinely pleased for her. "Your spring break is coming up soon, isn't it?"

"Yeah..." Jordan replies uneasily.

"Well, what would you think about a trip out of town with your dad and I? We've been talking about trying to get a place down on the Gulf like we used to when you were younger."

"I can't Mom," Jordan says. "I already have travel plans for the break. Sorry."

"Oh that's too bad," her mother answers, her tone clipped. "I assume you're going somewhere with that married man?"

"That married man has a name, and it's Chase," she snaps, irritated. "And I'd appreciate you not calling him that any longer. His divorce was finalized, so now he's a single as anyone else."

"No need to get testy," her mother says snippily, and instantly it is as if Jordan is fifteen again, disagreeing with her parents over a curfew.

"Actually, I think there's absolutely a need for it. You may not be thrilled about the choices I make, but I'm thirty-two years old and I have a right to make them the way I see fit!" Jordan can feel the fury rise up in her chest.

"Your father and I just don't want you to throw your life away on someone who clearly isn't good enough for you," her mother answers wearily.

Jordan knows that her parents are only trying to look out for her, but it's been more than two months, and her mind, they need to just get over it.

Instead of saying it though, she just sighs and says, "I don't want to talk about this anymore. Chase is in my life, and is an important part of it. If you can't be supportive of that, then I think it's for the best if you simply stop calling."

There is a long pause before her mother answers. "If that's what you'd like Jordan," she says.

"It is," she replies. "I have to go. Goodbye Mom," she says, ending the call without waiting for a response.

Jordan is reaching for her pen and list when her phone rings again. She reaches for it and answers without looking at the caller ID.

"Hello?" she says, her frustration clear in her voice.

"Hey Jordan," a familiar voice answers.

"Emmy, um, hi," she says hesitantly. Jordan hasn't heard it nor seen its speaker in nearly three months, but she recognized it instantly.

"How are you doing?" Emmy asks carefully.

"Things are good," Jordan responds tensely, unsure of where the conversation is going.

"That's good," Emmy replies equally uneasy.

"How are things with you?" Jordan asks.

"Things are good. Look, I didn't call to have weird small talk," her former roomate blurts suddenly. "I was wondering; could you meet me for coffee sometime? I don't like how things ended with us, and I really want to clear the air."

At any other time, Jordan might respond agreeably, but on the heels of the conversation with her mother, she just can't handle social niceties. "I think the air cleared pretty thoroughly when you moved out while I was out of town for Christmas," she answers.

"Okay," Emmy answers, "I suppose I had that coming to me."

"That's for damn sure," Jordan retorts.

"Jeez Jordan, can you just give me a chance to speak? I know I've made some really major mistakes, but I also know that I don't want to hash them all out over the phone. Can you please just meet me at the coffee shop across from campus tomorrow afternoon around four?"

Jordan pauses, trying to decide how to answer, when Emmy adds, "And don't try to tell me you have a class. I know you're done by three every day, and that you never do office hours on Fridays."

Jordan smiles in spite of herself. After so many years of friendship, there are things you just can't "un-know" about someone. "That sounds doable," she answers.

"Great," Emmy answers, relieved. "I'll see you

then."

"Bye," Jordan says before the phone disconnects. She looks around her room, eyes her packing list, and with a heavy sigh, she flops down on the bed. She lays there, staring off into the distance, until Chase comes home and finds her.

24 HARSH WORDS

Emmy arrives at the coffee shop ten minutes early. She's afraid that if Jordan gets there first and doesn't see Emmy, she will simply turn around and leave. It took her over a week of getting psyched up before she finally called Jordan and suggested this meeting, and she is desperate for it to go well. She nervously shreds the cardboard sleeve on her coffee cup as she watches the door out of the corner of her eye.

At four o'clock exactly the door to the coffee shop swings open, and Jordan walks in, glancing around the room until her eyes land on her. Emmy raises a hand in greeting, and Jordan nods in acknowledgement as she moves towards her table.

"How are you?" Emmy asks as Jordan removes her coat and drapes it across the back of her chair before sitting down.

"Good. Really good," Jordan replies. "How about you?"

"Things are going great at the shelter. It looks like

donations for our proposed expansion are all in order."

"That's wonderful," Jordan replies, smiling warmly at her. Then, a shadow passes over her eyes and she swallows. "So where are you living these days?"

Emmy pauses before answering, surprised that Jordan has brought up her relocation so quickly. "I got a little studio a few blocks from the shelter. It's tiny, but I'm saving a ton on gas money, and I really enjoy having some space all to myself."

Her words hang in the air and she immediately regrets saying them. Today is not about proving how well things are going now; it is about getting Jordan to understand why Emmy did what she did, and to see if there is any hope of repairing their friendship.

She tries to change the subject. "So how are your classes going this semester? Are you just about ready for Spring Break?"

Jordan exhales deeply and looks Emmy straight in the eye. "Listen Emmy," she says, "I know you didn't call me up after more than two months just to chit chat. So just tell me: what do you want?"

Emmy's gaze darts down to the table, and she pauses before answering.

"I just wanted to make sure that you're okay."

Jordan tries in vain to stifle a laugh. "Are you serious? You go completely nuts on me, you move out with no warning, *over Christmas*, and I don't hear a thing from you since? And now you want to know if I'm okay?" She narrows her eyes, and her next words send a chill down Emmy's spine.

"You're a judgmental bitch, and you completely

screwed me over. I came here hoping you might apologize, but clearly you are as sanctimonious as ever."

Emmy's eyes well up and she flinches as if each word is a slap. "Jordan, please, let me try to explain. I know that I left you in a horrible position, and I wanted to at least try to make you see why I did what I did. It might not make it right, but I'm hoping that you might one day be able to forgive me."

Jordan looks her straight in the eye, and Emmy can still feel the tears threatening to spill over. She tries to blink them away, but one escapes and runs down her cheek, and she quickly wipes it away. After a long silence, finally Jordan answers.

"Fine," she says flatly. "Give it your best shot Emmy."

She takes two slow deep breaths before beginning her story.

"I suppose it goes back to when I was younger. My dad cheated on my mom."

"I know," Jordan answers tensely, "but that doesn't mean you were right to react — "

"It's not just that. If it were just that he cheated, I might not see the world the way that I do," Emmy cuts her off. "You know that my parents split up when I was really young..."

"Yeah," Jordan replies. "You always said that your mom raised you by herself and you two never heard from your dad after he left."

"That's what I told you, but that's not the entire story," Emmy continues. "He *did* leave when I was little, and my mom *did* raise me herself. But I did have contact with him once, sophomore year of college."

At this admission, Jordan's eyes grow wide, and her expression softens with concern. "Emmy, you never told me."

"I know, and that was stupid of me Jordan, but I was so upset that I just couldn't share it with anyone, not even you. My dad sent me a letter, telling me that since I was over eighteen, child support was stopping. He also said that he was happy with his new wife and their sons, and that he wanted no further contact with my mother or me." Emmy's eyes are locked on Jordan's face, watching her process the information.

Finally, she continues her story. "Included with the letter was a check for five thousand dollars, which he said was to help with college expenses. Five thousand dollars was what his daughter, his firstborn, was worth. It felt like a payoff, a pity token to get rid of me."

Jordan's eyes are moist in the corners, and Emmy breathes a sigh of relief that she might just get through to her friend after all.

"All of this happened just a few weeks before you and Chase got together after exams. I just had this pit in my stomach, and I couldn't shake the thought that he was going to do the same thing to someone someday."

Emmy pauses, and continues her story. "The summer after sophomore year, my heart broke for you Jordan. He hurt you so much..." she trails off.

"That was more than a decade ago!" Jordan replies incredulously. "At some point, you've got to just let things go and allow people to grow up and change."

"But that's just the problem!" Emmy blurts loudly. "Chase DeWitt is never going to change. He was a serial cheater in college, and now he's a grown man cheating on his wife. Men like that never change, because women allow them to stay the same."

"You're wrong about that," Jordan snaps. "Chase has changed. He realized that his marriage was a mistake, and they've divorced."

Emmy's jaw hangs open in surprise for a moment, genuinely unable to come up with a response. She collects herself and exhales sharply, trying to stifle a snarky retort.

"Wow," she finally replies. "I can't say that I saw that coming."

"Well it did," Jordan answered primly. "Chase says that realized I was the one he is supposed to be with, so he moved into the spare bedroom in the apartment." She arches one eyebrow, silently reminding Emmy of exactly why the apartment had a vacancy.

Emmy cringes inside, though the steady expression on her face masks her feelings. A wave of nausea overtakes her at the thought of Chase DeWitt living in *her* apartment. She fumbles for an appropriate response, before saying, haltingly, "I hope the two of you are happy together." She pauses, and looks Jordan straight in the eye. "I really do. You deserve to be happy."

Jordan smiles, truly smiles, for the first time in the conversation. "Thank you Emmy. That means a lot to me."

"So things really are going well for you guys?" Emmy asks, determined to bring the conversation from a place of stress to one of peace, even if it means swallowing her knee-jerk reactions.

"Yeah!" Jordan answers brightly. "We are actually going on a trip together for Spring Break." Her ear to ear smile reflects the joyful tone in her voice.

Emmy smiles in spite of herself, her friend's joy is so palpable. "Sounds fun. Where are you guys headed?"

"Las Vegas," Jordan tells her. "I've never been, and he knows how much I love poker, so he arranged this amazing trip!"

"Well you two better be careful not to lose all your money," Emmy teases, and for the first time their friendship has their old easy back-and-forth again.

"Thanks man," Jordan replies, laughing.

Their conversation veers off on a tangent, talking about their jobs, mutual friends, and music. Emmy is glad that Chase is not mentioned again, and eventually they settle into a content silence.

Finally Jordan checks the time on her phone, and she raises her eyebrows.

"Damn Em!" she exclaims. "I've got to head on out. I have a stack of papers to finish grading before I can safely get into vacation mode."

Emmy smiles. "It's not a problem. I should be on my way as well. But I am glad we got a chance to catch up. I am truly sorry for how everything played out."

"It's alright," Jordan replies kindly. "Things work out the way they need to I guess."

She stands, and picks up her coffee cup. "I'll call you when I get back from vacation Emmy," she says.

"I mean it, Em," she adds when Emmy's face registers a hint of sadness. "It's going to be fine. I promise."

Emmy stands to give her friend a hug, and watches her walk away.

As Jordan disappears into the crowd, Emmy smiles, glad for how the afternoon has gone, and also anxious for how this will all turn out for her friend.

I hope that this all works out for you Jordan, she thinks to herself as she picks up her purse. *You deserve some happiness, and if Chase DeWitt is the one to give it to you, good for you.*

"Good luck Jordan," she whispers to herself as she tucks her earbuds into her ears and cues up a song. "I can't help but feel like you are going to need it girl."

25 VIVA LAS IMPULSE

"Oh shit!" Jordan exclaims from the bathroom.

"What's wrong?" Chase asks her.

Jordan whirls into the bedroom, her skirt flaring behind her and, without answering, proceeds to empty the contents of her makeup and toiletry bag onto their king-sized bed.

"Jesus Jordan! What the hell is going on?" he blurts in frustration.

"My birth control pills," she snaps back. "I must have left them in Atlanta!"

Chase sighs in relief. "Is that all? That's not a big deal Jor."

"Seriously?" she replies, her eyebrows raised. "Can you even imagine what would happen if I got pregnant?" She looks Chase straight in the eye, her left brow raised cynically.

"I wouldn't sweat it Jordan," he replies evenly. "There's little chance of that happening." He stretches, and wraps his long arms around her. "Don't worry for another minute. We're in Vegas, at the damn Bellagio for god's sake! Just enjoy it."

He begins to nuzzle her neck, and after a minute he feels her muscles unclench and she turns her head to meet him in a kiss.

Chase takes a few steps closer to the bed, leading her, and with a dramatic sweep of his arm he clears the bed. "Come on Jor'" he murmurs. "Let's start this trip off right."

***

As the sun is setting, Chase and Jordan finally venture out of their hotel room and make their way down to the casino. They settle in at a two-dollar blackjack table, because Jordan wants to save her real money for a few poker tournaments.

Within minutes of sitting down, a pretty cocktail waitress comes by to take their drink order. As she walks away, Chase cannot help but admire the way her short skirt sways across the top of her tan, lean thighs.

"Ahem!" coughs Jordan, shaking him out of his reverie.

"What?" he asks sharply, a note of irritation in his voice.

"It's on you," Jordan says. "I said your name three times, but clearly you are distracted. Hit or stay?"

He glances down at his cards. He has seventeen showing, an eight and a nine. The dealer has an eight showing, so he hesitates on his decision. Finally he glances up at the ceiling, shrugs his shoulders, and answers.

"Stay."

Chase looks at the other hands on the table. Jordan stopped at nineteen, an array of lower cards, and two other people have already busted out. The action moves to a middle-aged man to his right, and he busts out as well.

Finally the dealer, a sharp-looking, pleasant African-American man whose name tag reads "Jeff", turns over his hidden card, revealing a four. Jordan inhales sharply as he turns another card, and lets out a small squeal when it is six, giving him 18.

Johnny gives him a wink as he takes his chips and pushes Jordan her winnings. "Tough break man, Looks like the lady is off to a good start though," he comments.

"Yeah," Chase replies, placing a hand on Jordan's knee protectively. Suddenly the waitress is back with their cocktails, and he removes it again and runs it through his shaggy brown hair. He smiles at her as she hands him his drink, and he grins in return as he places two one-dollar chips on her tray as a tip.

"New hand!" declares Jeff, and Chase places his chips out for the next hand, then sneaks another glance of the waitress as she walks away.

They play about ten hands, approximately half of which he wins, while Jordan is nearly undefeated, losing only one hand.

"What do you say we go grab some dinner?" Chase asks.

Jordan turns to look at him and catches him fiddling with his keys. "Sure thing. I can tell you are getting a little antsy." She giggles and kisses his cheek.

Jordan collects up all the chips and dumps them

into her purse. "I don't want to cash them in until the end of the trip," she explains.

They get up from the table, but not before tipping Jeff a few one-dollar chips. Jordan reaches for his hand, and they stroll through the marble lobby of the Bellagio, marveling at the sculptures placed throughout.

"The décor in this place is amazing!" Jordan exclaims as they near the doors. "I've never seen anything like it before!"

"Wait until you see the rest of The Strip," Chase replies. "Las Vegas is one of my favorite places. There's always something to do or something to see."

"I know the whole thing is going to be amazing, but we're staying in the best place. Caesar's is a little cliché, and some of the other hotels are just plain tacky, but the Bellagio is straight-up gorgeous!"

He smiles and squeezes her hand. "I'm glad you're having fun Jordan."

"I'd be having a little more fun if you'd quit checking out the waitresses," she responds, sticking her tongue out. Her expression tries to convey that she's joking, but Chase can tell by her tone that she's irritated.

"Don't worry about it baby," he answers. "Vegas is a place to look, to gawk, and to take in. It doesn't mean that I'm not here with the most beautiful woman in the world."

He stops in the middle of the sliding doors that lead out to The Strip and sweeps Jordan up, planting a comically exaggerated smacking kiss on her lips. She sighs happily in his arms; they separate and continue walking, still holding hands.

"Wow," she exhales, taking in the full glitz of the city as they reach the sidewalk.

"I told you," is all Chase says in response, although one corner of his mouth turns up in a smirk.

He steers her down the street in the direction of Margaritaville, and laughs when she spots a group of girls carrying three-foot-long plastic tubes of some fruity mixed drink.

"I have got to get one of those while we're here!" she says eagerly. I can't believe they just walk down the street with them! You couldn't do that at home in Atlanta!"

"That's how Vegas works Jordan. You do things you would never do anywhere else," he tells her, smiling. "So what else is on your to-do list while we are here?"

"Gamble of course," Jordan replies instantly. "I'd love to play a hand or two of blackjack in as many casinos as possible. I can keep a one-dollar chip from each as a souvenir!"

"Well, I guess it's cheaper than buying a shot glass at each place,' Chase comments. "What else?"

"Well," Jordan begins, "I'd love to see a Cirque du Soleil show if you think we can get tickets. Also, I saw that our hotel has an art museum! How freaking cool is that? We've got to check it out!"

Chase groans, and then stifles it when he sees that she is absolutely serious. "I think I will be conveniently chilling out by the pool when it's time to do that one Jor."

She sighs and mutters an irritated-sounding "Fine. Are we almost to Margaritaville? I'm starving."

"Just a little bit further," Chase answers, ignoring

her moodiness. "Check it out--you can see the palm trees out front."

They walk into the restaurant and are, incredibly, instantly led to a table for two. Jimmy Buffet music blasts through the speaker system, and they simply nod at their waitress Jeanne when she recites the night's specials, not hearing a single word.

They both order the "Cheeseburger in Paradise" and the waitress scurries away. Chase's eyes once again wander, taking in Jeanne's taught midriff visible in her tied Hawaiian-print shirt.

"Good grief. Is every woman in Las Vegas drop-dead gorgeous?" Jordan exclaims.

Chase rolls his eyes. "What are you talking about babe?"

Jordan's eyes narrow, and answers, "You've been ogling every woman we've come across." She gestures to her pale white arms. "I can't compete with these girls! I'm an academic for crying out loud. My place is the classroom or the library."

Chase laughs, and answers, "Well, if it makes you that uncomfortable, you can join my gym when we get home. A few sessions with a trainer, maybe hit the tanning beds, and you'd be a bronzed hard-body in no time at all."

Jordan's jaw drops, and pain fills her eyes. "Is that what you really want me to be?" she asks, anxiety thick in her voice.

Chase pauses, knowing he has really put his foot in his mouth. "No Jordan," he replies. "I think you are absolutely beautiful and awesome just the way you are. Don't think about it for even a minute."

Her expression softens slightly, but Chase can still

hear the hurt in her response. "Are you sure though? I mean, you've known me for nearly fifteen years, and that's just not who I am."

She straightens her posture, head held high, and continues. "I mean, I make it a point to take care of myself, but if you want to be with a gym rat, that's never going to be me."

Chase takes her hand and smiles. "You are the woman I've wanted since I was eighteen Jordan Peck. You're the smartest person I know, and the sexiest." He picks up her hand a places a kiss on it. "You are the only one for me."

She sighs in relief, and smiles warmly at him.

At that moment, their waitress shows up with their drinks, and their conversation changes to what other sights they want to see. Jordan is so distracted she doesn't see Chase take one last peek as Jeanne walks away.

26 TO BE OR NOT TO BE

"All right guys," Jordan calls out as her freshman literature class begins. "Let's talk *Hamlet*."

She takes a long drink from her coffee mug, and wonders why she is so tired. She returned from Spring Break feeling refreshed, but over the last few weeks, she has grown increasingly fatigued. For the first time in her career, summer cannot come soon enough.

"Hamlet himself is a character made up of neuroses and contradictions. He is prone to grand declarations and then falters when it comes to backing them up with action," she begins, glancing around the room at her Freshman Literature students.

She continues. "In Act Two, a letter from Hamlet to Ophelia is read aloud. He states 'Doubt the stars are fire/ Doubt that the son doth move/ Doubt truth to be a liar/ But never doubt I love.' When you first read these lines, what did you think of Hamlet and his feelings for Ophelia?" She lets her gaze linger on her more outspoken students to prompt a response.

Lora, a small, quiet girl in the second row timidly raises her hand.

"Yes Lora?" Jordan asks, leaning in for the student's response.

"Well, initially I thought it was the most romantic thing I've ever heard," she begins cautiously.

"But?" Jordan questions, nodding for her to continue.

"But as the play continues, Hamlet treats Ophelia so badly!" she exclaims, furrowing her brow in frustration. "He swears his love for this girl, and eventually throws her aside, without ever explaining why."

Bradley, a more outspoken student, counters her. "Well think about everything he's going through at that point? His mom's a cheat and a killer! It's kind of hard to be a doting, attentive boyfriend when you're trying to unravel a murder plot."

"A valid point," Jordan concedes. She loves when her students get into intense debates in class. At times like this, she stops asking so many questions and just occasionally stirs the pot to keep them going.

Lora's irritation is written across her face. "But he could have *told* her! If Hamlet loved Ophelia, really loved her, wouldn't he own up to everything that's going on and turn to her for support?"

Bradley shrugs his shoulders in response, and smirks. "I'm a college freshman. What the hell do I know about love?"

"That excuse is a little weak when talking Hamlet, isn't it?" Lora retorts proudly. "I mean, Professor Peck, wasn't Hamlet basically our age when all of this was going on?"

Jordan smiles and answers the question, addressing the class as a whole. "Actually guys, Hamlet was thirty years old during the events of the play. That little detail is buried in a conversation with the gravedigger at the beginning of Act Five. So in reality, Hamlet was far closer to my age than he was to yours."

She looks around the room to a sea of surprised expressions. Lora's mouth actually hangs open a little in disbelief.

Jordan looks directly at the pale blonde girl, and says, "You're clearly surprised by this information Lora. Does this change your opinion of Hamlet at all?"

"Well, I think he still sucks," she blurts out. "I'm sorry Professor, but I really don't have a better word for it. I mean, he's *thirty*! Aren't people supposed to have it together a little bit better by that point? He sounds like an..." she pauses briefly, before finishing. "An overdramatic teenager! It's a little bit ridiculous, don't you think?"

"Well, trauma is trauma, but yes, Hamlet does seem to be a little regressive in his behavior, particularly as it concerns Ophelia," Jordan admits to the class.

James, a slim, African-American student in his early twenties, who confessed to Jordan at the beginning of the semester that he took several years off after high school to "get his act together and grow up a little" before matriculating, raises his hand. Jordan nods her head towards him, inviting him to speak.

"Well, I think that Hamlet is in the throes of young love, even if he is thirty years old."

"Go on," Jordan prompts.

"I think that Shakespeare wants us to assume that Ophelia is his first love, and because of that, he gets giddy and stupid and verbose in his declarations," James explains. "His earnestness indicates that he wants to mean all these things, but he's just so inexperienced and overwhelmed, that he doesn't know how to handle such a complex situation."

"Very good insight," Jordan replies warmly, and James grins proudly.

***

Later that afternoon, Jordan is practically falling asleep at her desk. Grading papers can get a little tedious, but she is having a hard time even keeping her eyes open.

I wish I knew what was wrong with me, she thinks to herself. She reaches into her purse for a stick of gum, hoping the act of chewing will make her a little more alert, and pulls out both a pack of gum and her birth control pills. She puts both on her desk in front of her, and slides the pack of pills out of their little plastic sleeve.

She is taking her placebo pills this week, and while she used to skip that week, once she and Chase started sleeping together, she starting taking the placebos as well, just to make sure she keeps on schedule.

"Oh shit," she whispers to herself.

Jordan looks at the pack of pills, and sees that she has taken five of the inactive pills, and her stomach churns as she realizes her period hasn't come yet.

In all the time she has been on birth control, it has always come on the second or third day of placebo pills. Jordan thinks about how tired she has been recently, her mind immediately starts racing.

There's no way, she thinks to herself. However, she cannot come up with another reasonable explanation.

Jordan stands up from her beat-up leather desk chair, and grabs her purse. She glances around the room quickly, sweeps some papers into her briefcase, and heads for the door, not even bothering to lock it behind her.

As she heads down three flights of stairs to her car, her mind begins running scenarios. If she is pregnant, and she stops to remind herself that she really doesn't know yet, what will she tell Chase? Furthermore, what will his reaction be? He has told her time and again that the "kid issue" was a major problem in his relationship with Kendra. More to the point, Jordan herself doesn't even know if she wants kids at all, let alone now, as she is preparing to start her doctoral program.

Her mind flits briefly to her other options if she is indeed pregnant, and she forces the thought out of her mind as she slides into her car. That situation is one she has never considered, never thought she would have to consider.

She tells herself that she doesn't need to let her mind go there until she knows for sure. She leaves campus and makes a beeline for the pharmacy down the street.

The bright fluorescent lights immediately give Jordan a headache as she heads for the ironically-named "Family Planning" aisle, as none of the things running through her head right now came from any kind of a plan.

She finds the "early results" tests, and splurges for a name brand three-pack, just so she can be absolutely sure. She walks nervously to checkout, casting furtive glances to make sure she doesn't run into any students.

As she pays the cashier, she briefly considers going into the store restroom to use the test. However, she resists, because if she is pregnant, she wants to make the discovery in the safety of her own home, where she can freak out in solitude.

She flips back and forth between radio stations on the drive home. She skips from classic rock to top forty pop, and even lingers on a country station for a few minutes, before the song playing becomes so twangy and over-dramatic that she slams the power button on the stereo. She makes the rest of the drive home in silence, her heart pounding with uncertainty.

When she pulls into the parking lot of her apartment building, she leaves her work things on the passenger seat, taking only her purse and the white plastic shopping bag containing the pregnancy tests.

Jordan takes the steps hurriedly; she is glad that Chase's job has him working late hours. For reasons she can't quite explain, she wants to handle this on her own, privately.

However, when she opens the door to the apartment, Chase, splayed out on the sofa, calls out to greet her.

"How was your day at work?" he asks as he crosses the small living room to give her a hug. His eyes dart down to the plastic bag.

"Ooh did you grab beer on the way home? I was going to text you that we were out!" he laughs, reaching for the bag.

"No!" Jordan shouts, jerking the arm holding the bag behind her back. She blushes at the intensity of her reaction.

Chase grins teasingly, and snatches the bag out her hands. "What are you hiding Jor?" he asks as he peers inside. He looks at her carefully, his eyes scrutinizing her harried expression. Suddenly his eyes get wide, and his expression changes from teasing to one of concern.

"Why do you have a pregnancy test?" he asks softly.

Jordan takes a deep breath and steels her nerves. "My period should have come a few days ago, and I have been absolutely exhausted for over a week. I don't think it's likely, because we are usually careful—"

"Except for Vegas," he finishes for her.

"Exactly," she breathes. "I just wanted to take a test to be sure. To figure it out one way or the other."

Chase's expression softens, and his smile returns. "That wouldn't be the worst thing in the world, would it?

Jordan's jaw drops, and for a moment, she remembers the look of disbelief on Lora's face in class earlier in the day, and she is sure she looks even more dumbstruck. "You've made it pretty clear that kids are not exactly in your life plan," she begins carefully.

Chase shrugs sheepishly, and Jordan marvels at how calm he is acting, when her whole body is wound up with stress.

"That was with Kendra," he says, smiling. "With you, I guess it would actually be pretty cool."

"What?" she shrieks. This was not the reaction Jordan was expecting at all.

"Think about it Jordan," Chase begins. "You and me, we're pretty awesome together, and if we brought a kid into the world, I think he would be pretty damn cool. Or she," he adds after a moment.

Jordan doesn't know how to respond to this, so she just stares at him, and twists the handle of the bag tightly around her fingers, cutting off the circulation and making her hand throb slightly.

Chase takes her silence as an invitation to continue speaking. "I mean, you're it Jordan. You're the girl for me, and I think we could really make a go of it. Just imagine if we got married and raised this baby as a family."

Jordan feels her anxiety, already sky high, rising even higher, and she knows that before this conversation, this incredibly insane conversation, continues, she first needs to take a pregnancy test.

She shakes her head vigorously, trying to clear her muddled thoughts from her mind. She looks at Chase. "I can't talk about this right now," she tells him, squeezing his hand. "I can't even think about any of it until I know for sure." Before he can reply, she hurries into her bathroom, their bathroom really, and opens the package.

She pulls down her grey trousers, then her panties, and she gasps when she sees a little bit of blood on them. She grabs the pregnancy test and pees on it anyway, because she remembers high school health class and knows that a little light spotting can still mean you're pregnant.

Jordan puts the cap back on the test, and sets it on the bathtub, and puts her head in her hands, bouncing on the balls of her feet as she waits for three minutes to pass before checking the test.

After what feels like an eternity, but has probably only been two minutes, she picks up the test.

The result is already in, and the digital screen clearly reads "Not Pregnant," and Jordan heaves a sigh of relief. She kicks off her work pants, grabs a tampon from the box under her sink, and gets herself composed. She splashes water on her face and changes into her favorite pair of pajama pants before finally walking back out into the living room.

"So what's the verdict? You preggers?" Chase quips, and Jordan feels a wave of irritation. She has spent the last hour and a half going out of her mind, and before even knowing the results, he is treating it like a joke.

"Actually, when I went into the bathroom, I found out my period started," she tells him curtly. "Then I took a test to be sure, and it was definitely negative."

Chase laughs and makes a show of banging his fist on his thigh. "Damn! I still think we could make some crazy cute babies. What do you say we go give it another shot?"

Jordan shakes her head. "I'm really sort of worn out from this whole day. I just want to go curl up in bed for a little while. Order whatever you want for dinner; I really don't care what we have. Just let me know when it gets here."

"Are you sure?" Chase asks, out of politeness.

"I'm sure. I just want to be by myself for a little while," she says, turning around to walk into the bedroom.

Jordan climbs underneath the navy blue comforter they purchased together when Chase started sharing her bed every night. As she pulls the blankets up under her chin, she thinks about his unexpected reaction. She knows that she should be thrilled about his enthusiasm, that it means he is genuinely serious about their relationship. However, she can't shake the knotted up feeling in her stomach, a sensation that has nothing to do with cramps.

She closes her eyes, but is unable to find sleep, her mind racing.

27 POOR IMPULSE CONTROL

Chase pulls into the mall and almost instantly realizes he is not destined to find a close parking space today, not on a busy Saturday such as this. He's parks in a spot toward the back of the lot, unsure what to do with this unexpected free afternoon, but Jordan warned him that morning that she had a stack of final essays to grade, so he needed to make himself scarce.

He figures the mall would be a good way to kill time: peruse the bookstore, get a haircut, and maybe get a present for Jordan. She has been so stressed lately; he thinks that a surprise gift might help her to mellow out.

Definitely, he thinks to himself. *A gift will be just the thing to snap her out of the mood she's been in lately.*

Getting out of his car, he whistles tunelessly to himself. Upon entering the gleaming white and chrome shopping mecca, he wanders about aimlessly, unable to focus long enough to select a store to walk into.

Finally, he finds himself standing in front of a jewelry store, the same one in which he looked for Jordan's Valentine's Day present, before deciding on the trip to Las Vegas.

"Given how that turned out, maybe I should have gone with jewelry," he mutters to himself, before entering the shop.

The glass counters, brightly lit and full of display pieces, line the walls of the shop and form an island in the center. Standing in the center of the island is a familiar face.

"Dawn right?" he asks the older woman, smiling warmly. Chase has always been good with names, and her beaming grin tells him he is right again. He strides over to her and asks, "How are you doing?"

Dawn's eyes crinkle at the corners as she replies, "I'm doing just fine young man. How sweet of you to remember me!"

He leans on the glass counter, eyes searching the contents within, as if waiting for inspiration to strike. Dawn asks, "So did you ever pick out a gift for that girlfriend of yours?"

Chase smiles again, pleased that she remembered their conversation so well. "I decided to take her on a trip, which worked out pretty well, but she's been under a lot of pressure lately, you know, with work and stuff, so I wanted to surprise her with something nice."

"Well isn't that thoughtful?" Dawn titters. She goes underneath the counter and pulls out a tray of simple silver bracelets. "We just got these in a few weeks ago, and they aren't particularly flashy. A nice starting point for a girl who's not a 'jewelry girl' perhaps?"

"Maybe," he replies, wandering down to a different counter, this one full of shining rings. "Can I get a closer look at some of the pieces in here?"

"Honey, those are our engagement rings," Dawn informs him. "Is that the direction your relationship is moving towards?"

Chase eyes the array of rings in the case. There are a few sapphires and a handful of pearls, but it's true, the majority of the rings in the case are indeed diamonds. They sparkle brightly under the display lights, and he smiles, imagining how Jordan's eyes do the same when she laughs.

"Honey?" the saleswoman asks him, breaking his reverie. "Is an engagement ring what you're looking for?"

It might be, he thinks to himself. "You know, I really think it is," he answers Dawn slowly. "I'm crazy about this girl, and we've been through some intense times together."

"Well, if that's the case, we've got plenty of beautiful rings that any woman would love," Dawn replies cheerfully. "What kind do you think that she would like?"

Chase pauses, unsure of how to answer. "I honestly don't know," he tells Dawn. "Probably a diamond, I guess. That's tradition right?"

"It is tradition," Dawn replies, "but if your girl isn't a traditional kind of woman, it may not be right for her. Some women prefer colored stones like emeralds, rubies, or pearls. I would recommend against an opal though, as it's supposed to be bad luck."

"I don't believe in bad luck," Chase smirks. "When

it's right it's right, and Jordan is definitely the right one."

Dawn smiles at this. "That's so sweet," she replies. "Let's see if we can't find just the right ring!"

Chase cannot help but grin in response. The more he stands in the jewelry store looking over the engagement rings, the more he feels his confidence rise. After the anxiety from her pregnancy scare a few weeks ago, Jordan has been keyed up and tense in a way that he has been unable to shake, no matter how much he jokes with or behaves affectionately toward her.

This is the perfect solution, he tells himself. He will be able to show Jordan in one single gesture how much she means to him. He hasn't even looked at another woman in weeks, and he believes in his heart that this is how everything was supposed to happen. Their affair, his divorce, the pregnancy scare, all of it has just been roadside stops on the way to this inevitable destination.

Chase grins widely at Dawn, and says, "You know what? I think the best thing to do is to bring her in with me to pick out a ring. I want to make sure it's exactly what she wants."

Dawn exhales sharply, and asks, "Are you sure that's the best idea?" She looks him straight in the eye. "In my experience, some women, especially the ones who don't see it coming, can react a little...dramatically," she finishes.

"No, I know that this is the right thing. It'll be perfect. Passionate and out-of-the-blue. She loves that kind of thing. One time I sent her flowers to her work, totally without warning, and she absolutely loved it."

The skeptical look on Dawn's face gives him a moment's pause. A bouquet of flowers isn't quite on the same level as a proposal, he has to admit, but Chase reassures himself that his idea is genius.

He shakes his head, as if trying to clear that small shred of doubt from his head. "I've got my plan Dawn. It'll be fantastic, and in a few days, you'll see us back in here to pick out her ring together. You'll see."

Dawn smiles, and wishes him luck, but her eyes are still clouded over with worry.

However, Chase doesn't take notice, as he is already on his way out of the store. He walks briskly to his car, gets behind the wheel, and takes off for the apartment he and Jordan share.

His pulse races as he cruises down the familiar roads, the wind tousling his hair. As he nears their apartment complex, he can't help drumming his hands on the steering wheel, nervous energy coursing through his body.

He pulls into the complex and slides his car into the spot next to Jordan's, and quickly hurries up the stairs to the third floor. At their door, he takes a second to straighten his blue button down and run a hand through his disheveled hair. He opens the door and steps inside.

"Hey there baby," he calls out to Jordan, dropping his keys and wallet on the dinette table.

"What are you doing back so soon?" Jordan's voice rings out from their bedroom.

"I..." he begins, then fumbles for the next words. "I just missed you baby. Needed to come home," he finishes awkwardly.

"That's sweet, but you know I'm swamped with grading," Jordan says, appearing in the doorway to their room, raking her fingers through her head and massaging her temples.

Chase takes a deep breath, and steadies himself for the words he is about to say. "Jordan," he begins, "I know you are incredibly busy, but I have to talk to you. It's really important."

Jordan's eyes go wide, and she bites her lip softly before responding. "What's wrong Chase?"

"It's nothing bad, but I needed to talk to you right away," he says quickly, striding across the room to wrap her up in his arms. He guides her over to the sofa then pulls at her gently until she is sitting down next to him.

"Chase, what is going on? You're starting to freak me out a little bit." Jordan looks up at him, her green eyes wide with alarm.

His hands immediately go to her, one cupping her chin, the other lightly stroking her hair.

"Baby, this isn't anything to worry about. In fact, it's a great thing. I wandering around this afternoon, trying to stay out of your way, and I had a revelation."

"A revelation?" Jordan's confusion is audible.

"Yes Jor. I realized something," Chase tells her, his confidence growing with each word he utters. "I realized that this is it for me."

Her confused expression matches her response. "What do you mean 'it'?" she asks him.

"What I mean baby is that you are the only person in the world for me. You are beautiful, brilliant, and the only thing I want," he tells her, smiling widely the entire time.

Jordan's eyes grow even wider, and she just stares at him for an uncomfortable moment before speaking. "What exactly are you getting at Chase?" she asks quietly.

"I want you to marry me Jordan," he blurts out excitedly. Jordan just sits, speechless, so he continues.

"What you and I have, it's incredible. I feel more comfortable, and happier, with you than I have with anyone else in my entire life. Let's take it to the next level Jordan. Please say you'll marry me." He smiles at her expectantly.

He watches her take slow, deep, breaths and furrow her brow, searching for an response. "Chase," she begins, "you're talking crazy. We've been together less than a year, and you only got divorced a few months ago. Think about it. Do you know how insane you sound?"

He continues, refusing to let her reaction derail his enthusiasm. "Seriously Jordan, we are absolutely perfect together. Can you think of a single real reason why we shouldn't be together for the rest of our lives?"

"How about the reasons I just laid out for you?" she blurts out in response. "We got together when you were married to another person. We've really only just started to figure out what our relationship is truly about."

Chase opens his mouth to respond, but Jordan cuts him off. "How about the fact that I very recently thought I might be pregnant, and your response was not at all what I expected?"

"You were just hormonal then Jordan," he tells her,

anxiety creeping into his voice. "It's not a big deal. We can have kids or not. You're call. I just really believe that you are the one I'm supposed to be with forever."

"You are not thinking things through," Jordan tells him, her voice shaking. "You act impulsively, and don't ever take the time to think through what the consequences of your actions are going to be."

She sighs deeply, and tears well up in her eyes. "It's what you've always done. With every relationship you've ever been in. Especially with me," she tells him softly.

"Jordan, baby, you don't know what you're saying," he murmurs as he reaches out for her. She shifts her body away from his touch, and he finally realizes, for the first time, that this conversation is not going at all the way he expected.

"What about all the arguments we've had? All the times one of us has gotten jealous? We're both guilty of it." Jordan asks him.

Chase pauses, weighing his response carefully. "Those were just growing pains baby. I love you, and we're supposed to be together. Ever since college, it's been you."

Tears escape Jordan's eyes and roll softly down her cheeks. "No Chase. It hasn't been me since college. If it were, then you would have been *with* me. There would have never been Kendra, or a parade of hook-ups. And there would have been no need for us to have an affair," she spits out the word, "because we would have been *together*."

His jaw drops open, as Jordan dissolves into tears on the sofa. His chest feels tight and his eyes begin to burn with tears that he tries to deny.

"Jordan, please don't talk like that. You know how special to me you are."

"No Chase," she answers him. "I know how much you love the things you can't have. Then you have them, and you immediately start looking for the next thing that you can't have. It's in your nature, and it has been as long as I've known you."

She pauses, and pulls up the hem of her t-shirt to wipe her eyes. "I think on some level, I've known this the entire time. I think that the person I am in love with is the person that you used to be. The eighteen year old boy who stole and then broke my heart."

"Jordan you don't really mean that, do you?" Chase asks, his voice cracking.

"I really do Chase. I'm so sorry. I feel like I've completely upended your life, and mine too to be honest, but this isn't the kind of relationship that life-long trust and love grows from."

She takes his hand in hers, and squeezes it tightly. "You are in my heart, and you always will be," she says quietly. "But I don't think that we can do this anymore. We don't trust each other, not completely, and given how this started, I don't think we ever will."

The tears Chase has been fighting back finally come free and slide down his cheeks. He glances at Jordan and sees a look of shock on her face. She has never seen him cry, as he very rarely ever does. At this moment though, he doesn't care how it looks or what Jordan thinks. He knows he is losing her, and it cuts him to his core.

Finally he works up the nerve to speak. "After all

that we've been through, that's really what it comes down to: the fact that you don't think you can trust me." It is not a question, just a statement of fact.

"It's the fact that we can't trust each other Chase. I know that saying it probably makes me a horrible person, but when I thought I might be pregnant, there was one thought I couldn't hold back."

"What's that?" he asks tremulously.

"All I could think about was how long it might be before you took up with another woman, and I was left at home, with a child, alone. Wondering when you'd come home," she finishes firmly but sadly.

Chase cannot stop the tears from falling, but in spite of this, he laughs. "What's so funny?" Jordan asks him.

"I'm nearly thirty-two years old, and this is the first time since high school that I've ever been dumped," he says wryly. "Besides Kendra," he adds. "But on some level, I kind of knew that one was coming."

Jordan laughs a little, but her face still shows her sadness. "I wish I could say it gets better, but no, it pretty much always sucks."

Chase looks at her longingly. "So what happens now? We share an apartment. How does this all end?"

"Well, I think for now, you start making use of the second bedroom," she says.

"That's my girl, always a smart aleck," he says, smirking.

"Seriously Chase," Jordan retorts, but her face also shows a hint of amusement. "We'll figure out the rest as quickly and painlessly as possible, but for now, that's the starting point. This whole situation is new to me to, as my last roommate took off suddenly and inexplicably," she adds, smiling at him. "We'll figure it out, and everything will turn out the way it's supposed to. I know it."

28 LIFE REBOOT

One year later…

Kendra Barnes, shakes her hair out after her evening yoga class, and gets ready to head out to meet the girls.

The last eighteen months have been a difficult period for her. First finding out about Chase's infidelity, then the subsequent ending of her marriage and reestablishing herself as a single woman has required her to adjust her priorities as well as how she sees herself in her head.

Finding a new place to live turned out to be the easy part. The house she and Chase had shared sold quickly, despite the realtor's warnings of how bad the housing market was. Kendra began renting a small apartment fifteen miles from her work, and other than the commute it has worked out very well.

She make good on her promise to Melanie, to go have an adventure. She spent nearly a month in Paris the summer after the divorce, taking in art museums and brushing up on her long-abandoned French studies from college.

Dating was something she avoided for over six months, until at the insistence of her friends she accepted an invitation out from Jesse, one of the fifth grade teachers at her school. While the date was pleasant, and was polite and charming, Kendra was still too raw, too shell-shocked from Chase's infidelity to pursue anything serious. She found herself preferring the comfort and solitude of her apartment to any kind of a social scene.

In recent months though, Kendra has found a place of peace with where she is at in her life. She has only a few more weeks left in the school year before summer vacation, and she finds herself unexpectedly excited for the break.

Last summer, she was still feeling the sting of the divorce, though she continually put on a brave face with her family and friends. However, now she feels prepared to really get on with her life.

She gets into her car, and heads over to Vinnie's, the wine bar that her friends love so dearly. A love song comes on the radio, and though months ago she would have reached for the controls to change the station, she now sings along loudly.

As her voice cracks as she reaches for a high note, Kendra can't help but laugh aloud. She has always been teased for her lack of vocal ability, and used to never sing aloud. "New Kendra," as she now thinks of herself, can't manage to be bothered with the self-consciousness that plagued her younger self.

She struggled for so long to fit the mold of the

perfect woman: wife, teacher, daughter, and friend. Now, she only worries about being good enough for Kendra, and that has made her life much easier, and admittedly, happier.

She pulls into the parking lot and smiles when she sees that her friends' cars are already there. She gets out and heads inside, ruffling her hair to shake out the tangles of the drive.

Melanie, Aubrey, Becca, and Alicia are occupying their favorite curved sofa, so Kendra drops down easily at the end. "How's it going ladies?" she asks warmly, glad to see her closest friends.

"Doing well Kendra," Alicia greets her warmly. "How are you doing?"

Kendra laughs a little, and then her laugh grows louder when she sees the look of surprise on her friends' faces. "Sorry guys," she says, still giggling. "Alicia just sounded so serious! I'm divorced, not dying."

Becca's expression is one of confusion. "But Kendra, you've been so down for so long! You hardly ever come out anymore, and we can't help but worry."

"I'm sorry guys," Kendra replies, her expression growing more serious. "It's been rough for a long time. Being out, being social, just didn't feel right."

"But you're feeling better now?" Melanie asks kindly, reaching out to squeeze Kendra's hand.

"I really am," Kendra answers firmly. "I'm the first to admit, it took me a long time to get here, and there are still days where I wake up and wonder how the heck I got here. But in general, overall, I'm good."

"That's great," Aubrey replies, grinning. "Becca's

been *dying* to badger you about when you are going to get back on the market."

"You bitch!" Becca interrupts, laughing. "It was absolutely your idea to try to set Kendra up with Mitch, the new associate at the firm. Don't go dragging my name into it."

"Ladies, ladies, there's no need to fight," Kendra giggles. "I know you all just want what's best for me." She pauses and looks around at the group of women in front of her. Her best friends, they may not be perfect, and they may have their moments where they drive her absolutely crazy, but they are at heart really good people.

"I'm not sure if I am ready to throw myself back into the dating world full force, but I am ready to keep my eyes open. If something interesting comes my way, I might just act on it." She smiles widely. "Now where is our server? After that, I need a drink."

As if summoned by magic, a tall, blonde-haired man, seemingly in his late twenties appears at the other end of the couch. "Welcome to Vinnie's," he says. "My name is Michael. What can I get you this evening?" He is incredibly good looking, and Kendra can help but smile widely at him.

"I'll take a glass of the house Shiraz," she answers. She cannot tear her eyes away from his classical features: strong jawline, elegant nose, and dark bristly eyelashes.

"Anything else I can get you?" Michael asks. "An appetizer perhaps?"

"How about your phone number?" Kendra asks slyly, trying to suppress her own surprise at her boldness. She looks past Michael quickly and smiles when she sees the look of disbelief on each one of her friends' faces.

Michael pauses for a second, then after second, smiles and answers her. "I think that we may have that particular item in stock. Let me go get you that wine and I will look into your 'special request.'"

Melanie waits until Michael is out of earshot before she blurts out, "Kendra Barnes! I have never seen you ask a guy for his number. Usually you just let them come to you." The rest of the girls nod in agreement.

Kendra smiles, and answers, "Well, a lot has changed. I'm not the same person I used to be."

"That's for sure," Alicia says, reaching out to give her a fist-bump, a gesture that she amazingly manages to make elegant. "I'm proud of you girl. And whatever happens, whether it's the waiter, or the guy from the Motormouth Twins' law firm, or someone else entirely, just know that we are here for you, no matter what."

"Thanks Alicia. That means a lot to me. I love you guys," Kendra replies, fighting back the tears of happiness that have suddenly sprung up in her eyes.

Suddenly, Michael has returned, with a large glass of red wine. He sets it down on the lacquered coffee table. "Your wine," he says, reaching into his front pocket for a folded slip of paper. "And here's the other item you inquired about," he adds, smiling warmly. "I sincerely hope you will make use of it."

As he turns to walk away, Melanie leads the girls in a slow clap in appreciation of Kendra's gutsy move. "I cannot believe that worked. You are so lucky!" she says, but her grin shows how happy she is for her friend.

"Who knows ladies," Kendra replies. "Maybe my luck is changing." She smiles and add, "About damn time!"

29 TURN THE PAGE

Chase slides into the seat across from Greg. It's only been a few days since they spoke last, but he hasn't seen his big brother in months.

"How's it going man?" Greg greets him.

"I'm doing alright," Chase replies, scanning the bar. "Been crazy busy at work, but I pulled a sick bonus this quarter, so I can't complain."

"That's good to hear," Greg replies. "I know you've been in free fall for a while, so it's nice to know that you are sort of settling down."

Chase pauses, and thinks to himself. After Jordan ended things with him, they both moved out of the apartment. Chase got a small sub-let near his office, and threw himself into his work.

For six months after Jordan broke up with him, Chase worked twelve hour days, soliciting new clients and producing content.

Eventually, he came out from his self-imposed solitude, and began to venture out into bars, tiptoeing into the dating scene. Once immersing himself back in the scene, his social life was fast and furious. He smiles, remembering the long string of girls he lost himself in.

As if reading his mind, Greg asks, "So how goes the Tour de Whore?"

Chase laughs at the nickname. "It's pretty much concluded. I've settled down a bit." It's true that when he finally got back out in the world, he had a series of one-night stands and short-term flings. For him, each woman was a diversion, a way to kill time, while he figured out what it was he really wanted.

Greg laughs then grows serious. "Good. You need to cut that shit out anyways. You're too old for crap like that" he admonishes.

"Hey, every girl I hooked up with, they knew the score," Chase says defensively. "I haven't deceived anyone, and I promise no hearts got broken in the process."

"Yeah, yeah, I've heard this from you before DeWitt," Greg replies, his expression still stern. "Seriously man, you need to cool it with the stunts and get focused on your future."

"I know, I know, I'm not getting any younger," Chase replies sarcastically. "Jeez, you sound like such a girl when you say things like that."

"I'm just looking out for you man," Greg answers defensively. "You're past thirty, time to put aside this kiddie crap and act like a man." He eyes Chase evenly and waits for his response.

Chase takes a moment to collect his thoughts. "You know what?" he begins. "I got married because I thought it was the 'man' thing to do. I wasn't ready for it. I did all kinds of shit to fill in the gaps in my life. Then the thing with Jordan started. I was happy, and I thought I had everything I ever wanted. Then she dumped me, because of the way I chose to fill in those holes."

"Chase calm down. I wasn't saying-"

"Yes you sure as hell were saying Greg. So now you'll shut up and listen," Chase snaps back, and Greg's face shows his shock at the cold tone in his voice.

"I'm just now finally feeling like myself again. And if it's alright with you, I am going to do what I think is right for me, right now. I'm not going to freak out worrying about my future, or if I'm going to die alone, or any of that crap. I am just going to worry about today. And tomorrow I'll worry about tomorrow."

Chase sighs deeply, the tension draining from his shoulders, "There's no way I can deal with the future right now Greg. I'm living day to day because that's all I can handle."

Greg looks at him, his brows knitted with worry. "So is that how it's going to be Chase? You just going to drift from girl to girl, never really laying down roots?"

"For now, yes," Chase replies. "Who knows? Maybe I'll meet someone and it all changes. Maybe I'll wind up married and deliriously happy. Maybe I'm a man whore until my dying day," he adds wryly.

Out of the corner of his eye, he spots an exotic-looking brunette walking into the bar. She is well-heeled, with well-tailored, obviously expensive clothes. Her dark hair swings loose around her shoulder. Chase watches her hips sway as she walks purposefully to one of the high top counters that encircle the main bar.

She sits down, alone, and pulls a book out of her bag. He catches the title, *Lolita*, and Chase can't help but smile to himself.

"Excuse me big brother, but I have something I need to do," he says, standing up from the table.

"Do what you think you need to do," Greg answers, sighing.

"Thanks, I will," he answers. He turns away from Greg and strides toward the reading woman. He stands in front of her, and she turns her head to look at him, her large, almond eyes glinting with curiosity.

He smiles his best smile and says, "Hey there, my name is Chase. What's yours?"

"Allison," she responds, smiling warmly.

"Good to meet you Allison. Might I say, that's a hell of a book you're reading."

30 FRESH INK

"That's going to be $250 dollars," the gruff man behind the counter says.

"All right," Jordan answers, handing him her credit card. "Can I do the tip in cash afterwards?"

"Yeah no problem," is his reply. "You got your design?"

Jordan reaches into her bag and pulls out a folded sheet of paper. "Yeah, here it is. Full color."

"Great. Let me go get your artist." The heavily pierced and tattooed cashier says before heading into the back area. Jordan looks nervously around the room while she waits. A minute later, he reappears, with a shorter, also tattooed man with a warm smile.

"Jordan?" he asks her.

"That's me," she replies carefully.

"I'm Johnny, and I will be the one doing your tattoo today. Is this your first time?" he asks.

Jordan can't help but laugh. "God, that's a funny way of phrasing it." He looks at her quizzically and she laughs even harder. "Sorry," she adds. "I guess you had to be there."

"No worries, I get a lot of first timers here. Don't sweat it. The whole process will take about two and a half hours, and you'll have a kick-ass new tattoo to show for your time." He smiles at her again, and Jordan can feel herself relaxing. "So what is it you're going to be getting today?"

"It's a phoenix," she says, unfolding the piece of paper. "Black outline with a red, orange, and yellow fade throughout."

"Beautiful design," Johnny says, and Jordan can't help but smile at his praise. This guy does tattoos day in and day out, and she is glad that she is getting something significant. "This is going to be a back piece right?" he asks her.

She nods. "Yeah, but I don't want it to start too low. I don't want to wind up with something that screams 'tramp stamp,' you know?"

Johnny laughs. "I know exactly what you're talking about. It's a pretty big piece, so we don't want to place it too high, but we'll make sure that no one equates to some nineteen year old girl with a butterfly right above her ass crack."

Jordan cannot hold back her grin. "That's exactly what I am hoping to avoid. Glad we're on the same page."

"Come on back. It'll take me a few minutes to get all my stuff together, but then we'll go ahead and get going on this thing." He leads her back to his station, and gestures to a folding chair. "Sit there, backwards, so that I can get to your back."

"Will do," she says, straddling the black metal

chair. She watches over her shoulder as Johnny lines up small containers of ink, and wraps a rubber band around the base of the tattoo gun.

"I'll be right back. Need to make a transfer of your design and we'll be ready to rock." Johnny walks back out front, and Kendra looks into the full-length mirror and bites her lip with nervousness.

Moments later, Johnny reappears. "Pull your shirt up and tuck the back under your bra. That way it won't fall down while I'm working."

Jordan follows his instructions, then sits motionless as he applies the transfer of her tattoo onto her back.

"Stand up," he instructs her, "and make sure the placement is okay."

She looks in the full-length mirror at the image. The tail feathers of the phoenix hit her lower back, but the body of the creature extends up and its wings reach across her back, each ending just a few inches from her side.

"It looks perfect," she tells him.

"Great," the artist replies. "Have a seat and we'll get started."

Jordan settles back into the chair, and draws a short breath.

"You nervous?" Johnny asks.

"Just a little," Jordan admits, giggling. "Is it that obvious?"

"Well, I've been at this a little while," Johnny admits. "But most people, when they come in for a first tattoo, they get something small. With women, it's usually something on the hipbone or ankle. This is a pretty serious tattoo for a newbie."

Jordan laughs. "Well, I feel pretty serious about it,

so I guess that's appropriate."

Johnny presses down on the trigger of the tattoo gun, and Jordan jumps slightly when she hears the buzz. "This is what it's going to sound like, so get used to the noise." He presses the trigger again and this time Jordan maintains her composure. "Good girl. Arch your back over the chair, and I'm going to get started. I'll do a short line first."

Jordan exhales slowly, then tells him, "I'm ready."

She feels the scrape of the needle on her back, a completely foreign sensation, but while she expected it to hurt, instead it feels oddly soothing, as if the events of the last two years, ever since the conversation with Chase that changed everything, are being scraped away and replaced with this new content.

Johnny is the first to break the silence. "So what motivated you to get a phoenix? There a story there?"

Jordan glances up and catches her reflection in the mirror. "You could say that," she answers, smirking.

"Well, we're going to be here awhile. Tell as much as you like."

Jordan pauses before answering. How could she possibly sum up everything that happened with Chase, their entire relationship, the damage to her friendship with Emmy, in just a couple of sentences?

"I guess, the easiest way to describe it," she begins, "is that I have been through a lot of stuff in the last few years, you know, emotionally. And after making some really tough decisions, I feel like I am finally in the place I am supposed to be."

"And where is that?" Johnny asks, as he continues to work.

"Well, I teach literature classes for a small university, and I am just about to start my second year of my doctoral studies," Jordan begins, "but it's more than that." She pauses.

"About a year ago, I had to do a 'life reboot' of sorts. There were elements in my life that weren't good for me, and even though it hurt like hell, I had to get rid of them. Then I had to go and look at the parts of my life I had been disregarding and try to put those pieces back together."

"Sounds intense," Johnny replies.

"It was," Jordan admits. "There were a lot of things I didn't do right, but in the end, I feel like I gained, I don't know, wisdom I guess. There are parts of your past that belong in your past for a reason. Sometimes the best thing you can do is leave them there."

"This next part is going to hit right over your ribs, and it may sting a bit. Just stay still," Johnny warns. "Seems to me like you must be a pretty smart professor," he adds.

"Jordan laughs in spite of herself. "I'm trying," she admits. "There are a ton of things I don't know, but I feel like I am more aware of it now, and can deal with it better. Hence the phoenix." She smirks at herself in the mirror.

"I guess I am being reborn as a more 'with-it' kind of person," she adds.

"That sounds fascinating, and I'm not even done with your outline yet," replies Johnny. "First rule about tattoo artists—we gossip more than teenage girls. So go ahead, give me the whole story."

Over the next two hours, that's exactly what Jordan does. She tells about her history with Chase as the outline is finished, then goes into the details of their relationship, and all of the damage and joy it brought with it, while Johnny fills in the color.

Finally, she comes to the ending. Breaking up with Chase and starting over. She tells him about how hard it was to end things, but how relieved she was when it was over. How she immersed herself in teaching and her own schoolwork while she healed.

"Almost done," Johnny comments. "Just doing some touch-up."

Jordan exhales slowly, trying note to move, though her back has grown rather stiff as she held her position.

"So what's your situation now? You dating?" Johnny asks. He gestures to a simple gold band on his ring finger. "I've been married ten years, and I couldn't imagine being out in the dating world now."

Jordan smiles. "As a matter of fact, I have had few dates in the last several weeks. It's still really new, but I'm enjoying myself, and I don't feel overwhelmed by past baggage."

"Sounds great," Johnny replies. "Some guy from your school? Or is it some professor with leather patches on the elbows of his coat?" he asks. "Also, I just finished up. Stand up and take a look."

"Actually, it's neither of those," Jordan answers, standing up and arching her back, working out the stiffness that has settled in during the tattoo.

She twists to look at the reflection of Johnny's handiwork. The colors blend together beautifully, and the line-work is crisp.

"It's beautiful," she says softly.

"Glad you like," Johnny answers. Jordan reaches

into her wallet and pulls out three crisp twenty dollar bills.

"These are for you," she says, pressing the bills into Johnny's hands. "This turned out even better than I could have hoped. Thank you."

"You're most welcome," Johnny says, smiling. "By the way, if he's not a professor or a budding doctor of literature, who's the guy?"

Jordan smiles before answering. "Just a guy my parent's recommended. They're friends with his parents. His name is Caleb." She walks to the door, pauses, and turns around to look at Johnny one last time.

"So far, he seems like a really good guy. If things don't work out, I'll just start over. Pick up the pieces and keep going. I did it before, and I'm still here right?"

She pauses, and smiles broadly. "Regardless of how it all works out though, right now, I'm happy. Isn't that what matters?"

ACKNOWLEDGEMENTS

There are so many people to thank. This has truly been a labor of love for almost a year and a half, and without the support of the people around me, I don't know if *When It's Broke, It's Perfect* would have ever seen the light of day.

First off, to the person holding this book, thank you for taking a chance on an untested author, and I hope you enjoyed reading my work as much as I did writing it.

Greg Wallace, for being there from conception to publication, holding my hand and watching me tear my hair out (metaphorically speaking, of course). Thank you for being my sounding board and second pair of eyes.

Michael A. Goodwin, for being my third pair of eyes and a trusted mentor. He came in late to this project, but offered counsel and tech support when I needed it most.

Joe Peacock, for teaching me the ins and outs of self-publishing, and reminding me that I was a badass, and not a lunatic, for even trying.

Randy Crump, Robert Hornback, and Bill Brightman, for teaching me how to be a better reader, a better writer, and a more thorough observer of humanity.

My entire family, especially those who aided in my

fundraising efforts: Ed Apsey, Chris Dowling, Ian Dowling, Peter Dowling, TJ Dowling, Don Hunter, Jeanne Hunter, and Lora Wall

All my amazing Kickstarter backers, but most especially- Dane Andrade Kim Bundschu, Anna Chopra, Kelly Cogan, Josh Copland, Andrew Dirks, Elizabeth Falkenberg, Joanne Howard, Brian Jones, Jake Martinsek, Craig Merriman, Michael Miller, John Moale, Bryan Pittard, Lora Sharp, Joanne Trew, and Becky Winget.

My parents, Mark and Pattie Bagley, for never once losing faith in me, even when I had to retake math in college.

My Geeklings, my precious Tiny Humans, who will on occasion quiet down long enough for me to edit my work.

Finally, the largest thanks of all goes to the man who has supported me day in and day out, every step of this journey, my husband Trevor Dowling. His steadfast belief in me kept me sane when I was otherwise ready to swan dive off the deep end. Thank you thank you thank you. You are, and will always be, "The Special."

QUESTIONS WITH ANGIE DOWLING

Where do you come up with your ideas?

Quite frankly, a lot of my ideas, including the one for this novel, come from things I overhear. I'm an unrepentant eavesdropper, but since I rarely hear the entire conversation, it gives me a fascinating starting point for my stories.

It also helps that I am a magnet for crazy. I leave my house and the madness just finds me. The next piece I am working on is inspired by some of the more recent shenanigans to cross my view.

What made you get into writing?

I've wanted to be a writer since I was ten years old. My parents got their first computer, and I typed a Christmas-themed short story in Note Pad. It was also my first foray into formatting.

I've kept a journal since middle school, and find it cathartic to just take whatever is bouncing around in my head and put it on the page.

Who is the author that most inspires you?

Douglas Coupland is both my favorite author to read and my "author-idol". His debut novel *Generation X* is in my mind the most perfect piece of fiction ever.

What is your writing process?

This novel developed with a lot more structure than anything I've ever worked on previously. To be honest, I think my structure helped keep me on track. When I first latched onto the concept, I started theorizing possible ways the scenario could work out. I spent an entire day at the Warped Tour with my friend and editor Greg, and realized I had a lot of ideas, and could really develop it into a novel.

Once I sat down to start writing, I first outlined my basic plot. Then I drew up rough biographical sketches of my main characters: first Jordan, then Chase, then Kendra. Emmy, Melanie and the others came later, although I had the idea for the "Emmy character" pretty early on.

Next I drew up an outline of the entire novel. It broke down the entire story into chapters and established key plot points and the point-of-view character for each chapter. Much of this changed over time, but the infrastructure helped me stay organized.

Once I had a basic skeleton of the story, I just sort of threw myself in. The early pieces needed a *lot* of rewriting, but I got a grip on the characters' voices pretty quickly.

How often do you sit down to write?

I attempt to do some writing every day, but after a full day in the classroom and life with three kids, it doesn't always work out that way. I make a point to dedicate four to five hours straight of writing at least twice a week though.

How do you know if what you write is any good?

I am pretty lucky in the fact that I have many friends who are both well-read and unabashedly honest. I use them as my first test group, along with posting some things on the internet for feedback. I am also not afraid to hand my work over to a stranger or near-stranger and see if it hooks their attention. If the response is good, it fuels my confidence. At the end of it all though, I tend to trust my gut. It rarely steers me wrong.

What is one thing you would change about your writing style?

I would use less profanity in my dialogue. I probably swear more than I should in my own life, and it seems to just seep its way into the conversations between my characters.

When you went back to edit, did you make any changes knowing that your mother and grandmother would read it?

See my previous answer! While my core content has stayed the same, I did have to go back and "watch my language". The final draft has about 70% less swearing than my initial version! Sorry Mom and Dad!

Where do you write?

I prefer to write in places that are semi-crowded, which I know is pretty weird. When it's too quiet, I have a hard time focusing. Plus when I have a bunch of people around me, I can always eavesdrop and come up with new ideas.

What advice do you have for people who want to get started writing?

Just write. Put pencil to paper, fingers to keyboard, whatever it takes. Whether it's just a recounting of your day or an observation of some random thing you saw or heard, record it. Finding your story can be more complicated, but if you want to be a writer, just write.

At what rate of hourly caffeine ingestion do you find writing easiest?

I actually don't like drinking a lot of caffeine when I write. I tend to get a little hyperactive (and I can hear my friends laugh as they read this), and I need to keep a certain degree of focus.

What is your writing playlist?

Music is a huge passion for me, so I usually write with my headphones in. Over the last year and a half, a lot of songs and/or bands have made their way onto my iPod as I work.

I find that listening to Broadway showtunes is especially helpful when I'm working on broad plot components, especially ones with great pacing.

When working on particularly tense scenes with lots of dialogue, I make a point to try to tap into some song among the 6,000 in my possession that fits the mood of what I am working on.

When all else fails, I throw on something bouncy and energetic, and just let it set the pace for how quick I type. Then, after a few songs, I go back and see what I came up with.

This is a partial list of the songs that either fueled me or remind me of certain characters or moments.

"Girl for Tonight" by MEST- Chase's theme song.

Dirty Work and *Don't Panic* by All Time Low-upbeat music with great lyrics, perfect to listen to while cranking out a chapter.

"Legendary" by The Summer Set- Jordan's theme.

"Right Brain/Left Brain" by Bo Burnham- This is actually a comedy piece, but I saw him perform it live about a year into this project. The whole thing is a battle between cold logic and unbridled impulse. I think it describes Jordan's struggle early in the novel.

"Deer in the Headlights" by Owl City- This is how Jordan feels when she realizes Chase's feelings at the end of the novel.

"Farther Down" by Matthew Sweet- Jordan's song when she is missing Chase.

Save Rock and Roll by Fall Out Boy- I feel like the tracks from this album, especially "Alone Together," "Just One Yesterday," and "Young Volcanoes" could stand as the soundtrack to the entire novel.

"I Found Away" and "Another Innocent Girl" by Alkaline Trio- Two more songs that remind me of Jordan, courtesy of my favorite band.

"You Make Me Feel So" by Cobra Starship- Fits Jordan's feelings for Chase early in the novel.

"Make It Last" by Stroke 9- Anthem for Chase and Jordan during the early part of their affair.

"Kiss Off" by Violent Femmes- This song embodies Kendra's mindset once she kicks Chase to the curb, even though I feel it is a genre of music she would hate.

"One More Night" by Maroon 5- This sums up Chase's feelings when Jordan breaks up with him.

"Here I Am Alive" by Yellowcard- This is Jordan's song at the end of the novel.

ABOUT THE AUTHOR

Angie Dowling was born and raised in the suburbs of Atlanta, Georgia. A child of artists, and a life-long geek, she dreamed of being an author since age ten. She earned a Bachelor's degree in English from Oglethorpe University, and a Master's degree in Secondary English Education from Georgia State University, both in Atlanta.
She currently lives and teaches high school in a suburb of Atlanta. She and her husband Trevor are the proud parents of three incredible Tiny Humans known affectionately as The Geeklings.
This is her first novel.